Manolito Four-Eyes

The 3rd Volume of
the Great Encyclopedia of My Life

Manolito
Four-Eyes

The 3rd Volume of
the Great Encyclopedia of My Life

BY ELVIRA LINDO

ILLUSTRATED BY EMILIO URBERUAGA

TRANSLATED BY CAROLINE TRAVALIA

MARSHALL CAVENDISH CHILDREN

Marshall Cavendish Corporation
99 White Plains Road
Tarrytown, NY 10591
www.marshallcavendish.us/kids

This book is a work of fiction. Names, characters, places, and incidents are products of the author's imagination and are used fictitiously. Any resemblance to actual events or locales or persons, living or dead, is entirely coincidental.

Library of Congress Cataloging-in-Publication Data
Lindo, Elvira
[Como molo. English]
The third volume of the great encyclopedia of my life / by Elvira Lindo ; illustrated by Emilio Urberuaga ; translated by Caroline Travalia.
p. cm. — (Manolito Four-Eyes)
Summary: Recounts the further adventures of the resourceful Manolito and his friends while on summer vacation in the Madrid neighborhood where they all live.
ISBN 978-0-7614-5651-3
[1. Family life—Spain—Fiction. 2. Friendship—Fiction. 3. Spain—Fiction.] I. Urberuaga, Emilio, ill. II. Travalia, Caroline. III. Title.
PZ7.L65911Th 2010
[Fic]—dc22
2009004350

Book design by Jay Colvin
Editor: Robin Benjamin

Printed in China (E)
10 9 8 7 6 5 4 3 2 1

Marshall Cavendish
Children

To Laura San José, may her smile always be beautiful, and to Cesítar Lindo Junior, may he think of me from so far away

CAST OF CHARACTERS

Manolito Four-Eyes
A ten-year-old boy from
Carabanchel, he's a chatterbox
who's misunderstood.

Grandpa Nicolás
Manolito's unconditional ally

The Bozo
Manolito's favorite little
brother—he only has one!

The One-and-Only Susana

This girl is like a whirlwind. Her limitless imagination can get anyone in trouble, especially Manolito.

Ozzy

The biggest bully and troublemaker in Manolito's school

Big Ears

A despicable traitor and Manolito's inseparable friend

Miss Asunción

Even though she thinks all her students are delinquents, she never loses hope that they'll change.

Also Available

Manolito Four-Eyes

Manolito Four-Eyes: The 2nd Volume of the Great Encyclopedia of My Life

Manolito Four-Eyes

The 3rd Volume of
the Great Encyclopedia of My Life

The other day, we were playing in an open field that's right next to the Carabanchel jail, when a car pulled up and slammed on the brakes so hard that the wheels skidded. I thought, you know, the normal thing, that they'd come to kidnap, rob, or bribe us so we'd keep quiet. Just in case, I got behind my little brother, the Bozo, because my survival instincts are great, and I do whatever it takes to save my own skin in difficult situations. We all froze: Ozzy the Bully, Arturo Román, Paquito Medina, Big Ears López. The Bozo's pacifier was the only thing that could be heard, because when he gets nervous, the number of sucks per minute increases.

In the cloud of dust where the car skidded to a stop, we thought we saw a Hobbit appear. As you can imagine, our eyes were about to pop out of their sockets. When the dust cleared, we realized it wasn't a Hobbit, but a kid. He stood there in front of us, not knowing what to say. Then a man who must've been his dad got out of the car and said to him, "C'mon, we've been looking for him all morning, and now you're just going to stand there and not say anything?"

All of our minds wondered, "Looking for who?"

Finally, the kid got up the courage to speak:

"I'm looking for Manolito Four-Eyes."

My friends all pointed at me. Even the Bozo took his pacifier out of his mouth and pointed with it. They're like me—their survival instincts are highly developed—and they're capable of turning over their best friend (or brother) to a total stranger if necessary. Just like I am. And it's not because they don't love their friend (or brother). It's because the famous survival instincts begin with yourself.

Anyway, it was easy to guess who Four-Eyes was, since I'm the only one in my posse that wears glasses.

"Yeah, so I've read the book all about you, *The 2nd Volume of the Great Encyclopedia of My Life*, and I had a couple of questions," said the kid, and he took a piece of paper out of his pocket.

These were the kid's questions:

1. Why do you call the Bozo "the Bozo"?

2. How long have you worn glasses?

3. Has no one ever defended you from the attacks of Ozzy the Bully?

4. What is Big Ears López's real name?

5. Why do you guys call the park "Hangman's Park"?

6. Why is Bernabé your godfather? Why is Our Nosy Neighbor Luisa always running the show in your apartment?

7. Why is Susana called "the One-and-Only"?

8. Does the Oscar Mayer hot dog factory belong to the dad of that kid in your class with the same name?

9. If Big Ears is your best friend, why do you say he's a dirty traitor?

10. Could you explain exactly what a "delayed-reaction lecture" is and why your mom is so good at giving them?

11. When did your grandpa Nicolás get his first dentures?

12. How did Jessica the ex-Fat Fatty lose weight?

13. Why is your dad never home?

14. Did Our Nosy Neighbor Luisa buy her dog, Miss Bonnie, or did she find her in some dumpster?

I won't go on because the kid brought like fifty questions with him. That kid was from another neighborhood, and he came to mine just to clear up some of the doubts he had; well, and also, I gotta admit, because he had an aunt in Carabanchel. I told the kid the best thing he could do was read the first volume of my biography. And that soon he'd be able to read the third one (that's this one, by the way). I also told him that there were some questions that nobody, not even me, could answer, like why the One-and-Only Susana's underpants were always dirty, because that's the type of question that not even the world's scientists can answer. Then Ozzy, who was green with uncontainable envy because I was the center of attention for once, told the kid:

"Nobody here has gotta read all of Four-Eyes' books. Heck, I gotta look at him every day, and that's enough for me."

The kid said, "Is this Ozzy?"

"How did you know?" asked Big Ears, whose mental coordination is a little slow.

"And you're Big Ears."

"He's got psychic powers!" said Big Ears. (I think he still doesn't know why we call him Big Ears.)

"And the guy who's wearing the Rayo Vallecano T-shirt is Paquito Medina," the psychic kid went on.

The Bozo was in such awe that he opened his mouth so wide his pacifier fell on the ground. He wiped it on my pants and put it back in his mouth.

"And this is your brother, the—"

"The baby," the Bozo interrupted him.

"He only likes it when *I* call him the Bozo, 'cause I'm his brother and his leader," I said.

"And who's that?" asked the kid, pointing.

"It's Mustard, my new lifelong friend. In the third book, there's a whole chapter dedicated to him. And, yes, that's his real name."

"Mustard's got a lotta nerve. He shows up last and gets to be in the book more than anyone," complained Arturo Román.

The psychic kid also knew that the one who had just talked was Arturo Román, because he's always complaining about stuff like that. The kid told me that he would like to see for himself if my grandpa is as funny as I said, if Bernabé's toupee is as noticeable as I said, if it's true that Our Nosy Neighbor Luisa and Miss Bonnie really look like identical twins, if my mom's lectures exceed his mom's in terms of skill and sophistication, and above all, that it would be a whole lotta cool if my dad let him climb into his truck (which is also named Manolito) at night, with the headlights on, and let him honk the deafening horn. But then the mysterious kid's dad yelled from the car that it was getting late. Before the kid left, he asked, "In the next book, could you make a list of all the characters and tell who they are so that people don't get mixed up? *Adiós, amigo.*"

His dad drove by us, creating another big cloud of dust. The strange kid disappeared in the smoke. Then the car drove away so fast that sometimes, when we think back on it, we're sure that it was a supernatural event, one of those paranormal phenomena that are so common in Carabanchel and that attract scholars with goatees from all over the world to our neighborhood.

Thanks to my new nameless friend, I realized that ever since I started telling my life story, I have a lot more

friends than I could've ever imagined, even if I haven't seen their faces and I don't know their names.

I wrote the full list of names he asked for. Paquito Medina helped me do it, and he said it was called a "family tree," which is this thing that kings or people like me, who are interested in history, should have.

In the branch dedicated to my friends, there's an open space. I like to say that your best friends are the ones you haven't met yet.

FAMILY TREE

1. The beginning of time

2. A few years after the beginning of time . . .

3. A Manolito on wheels

4. Me and the King of the house

5. Our Nosy Neighbor Luisa, my godfather Bernabé, and Miss Bonnie, almost a daughter to them, almost a cousin to me

6. My uncle Nicolás and his girlfriend from Norway

7. My best friend, Big Ears López, a dirty traitor with psychological problems

8. Ozzy, a problematic bully

9. The One-and-Only Susana, an X-File

10. Mustard, the dentist of the opera

11. Paquito Medina, who's so perfect he's out of this (worldwide) world

12. You

13. Miss Asunción, a.k.a. Our Teach, the director of the penal institution where I study (a.k.a. school)

1

Like Millionaires

At the end of the school year, when I brought home my report card, my mom only noticed the big fat F that Miss Asunción gave me in math. She could've cared less about all the rest of the grades. She ran out to cry to Our Nosy Neighbor Luisa, and my grandpa said, "Your mom chose the wrong profession. She should've been an actress."

For the next few days my mom looked at me resentfully, reminding me every second how silly I was for failing such an easy subject. She was so mad at me that the day Luisa left to go to her summer "mansion" in Miraflores de la Sierra, my mom said to her, loud enough so that I could hear, "Well, we're not going anywhere because of this little guy, who has kept me and his dad up at night worrying about his F."

I felt real bad for keeping them up at night, staring at the ceiling in silence and thinking about their son, who can't memorize his multiplication tables. I especially hate the nine table; I wouldn't wish it on anyone, not even my worst enemy.

I went over to the corner behind the minibar and started crying (I started crying kind of loud so they could hear me; crying by yourself when no one can hear is a waste of time). When my mom came to get me awhile later, I was a completely grief-stricken child, my eyes full of tears and my nose full of snot. Even the most insensitive person on the planet (my mom) should've felt sorry for me, but the only thing she said was, "Well, son, that's it for our summer, but don't worry, you'll always have your family to help you through all your failures."

"My little angel," my grandpa said, taking me into his arms. I cried even harder because, as you can see, it was a pretty tragic scene.

Seeing the effect of her horrible words, my mom confessed that the real reason we weren't going anywhere wasn't because of my F, but because we had to make some payments on my dad's truck and we didn't have any money left over to go on vacation. Then she started crying, and she begged me not to tell Luisa, because she was sick and tired of Luisa bragging about her colossal mansion in Miraflores de la *whatever*. It makes my mom sad that we never have money to go on vacation, but she doesn't want anyone to know, so she tells all the neighbors big fat lies; when it's not me and my grades, it's my grandpa and his prostate problem or the Bozo who's got a new fang coming in. She has forbidden me to talk to anyone about the money we still owe on the truck. It's too bad because up until now, I've been going around every month telling the neighbors how much money my parents have.

I know how much money they have because every night my parents go over their finances, and I record everything in my brain. But now I can't talk about that great topic: money. And Our Nosy Neighbor Luisa asks me about it all the time. Too bad. I love to talk about money. Maybe when I grow up I'm going to be an important banker, or maybe I'll end up kind of poor like my parents.

So, back to what I was saying: my mom started crying. It must've been contagious because soon my grandpa and the Bozo were crying, too. (They'd probably join her if she were standing in front of a firing squad.)

We all ended up hugging, wiping each other's noses with the same tissue (to save money), and thinking about my dad. At that moment, he was probably making some delivery in order to earn money to pay off our famous truck. Our debt on the truck won't be paid off until 2050, so my parents will leave me the debt in their will, and it's very possible that I will leave it to my own kids as part of their inheritance. The García Moreno inheritance is not

like the ones in the movies. It's the kind of inheritance that ruins your life.

I was glad that my mom told me the real reason we weren't going on vacation. It made me feel a whole lot better knowing I wasn't the main cause of my family's misfortune. The truth is, my mom didn't go around ridiculing me in front of that many people. You gotta be thankful when your mom shows some restraint. Now that I think about it, she really didn't have many opportunities to tell people because, like every summer, we were the only ones left on this side of the Manzanares River, which is the river that runs through Madrid.

My good friend Big Ears López was the first one to disappear (you know, the dirty traitor). Since his parents are divorced, he goes with his dad in July to a town called Carcagente. Then, at the end of the month, he comes back to Carabanchel, and on August 1 he goes with his mom to a town called Carcagente. Why, you might ask? Because it's the same town. His parents are both from Carcagente, but they go during different months because they can't stand each other. Two weeks after Big Ears left, he sent me a letter:

Dear Manolito, by the time the summer's over I'm going to have Carcagente coming out of my ears. There's a pool here but yesterday it rained.
Bye,
B. E. López

That's my friend for you: affectionate and expressive. It took him two weeks to write these two unforgettable sentences.

I wish I had a town to go to; even if it were Carcagente, I wouldn't care. One of those towns where you can walk out of your house and roll around in the fields until dawn, and you can sleep over at any house you feel like. You see a house with its door open and you go, "I think I'll take a load off here," and in that house there lives a woman who's pretty nice, and she makes you dinner, lets you watch TV, and then goes to talk to your mom and says, "Please don't yell at your son for disappearing. He's made me and my poor old husband, who can't hear and can hardly see, so happy."

That's what's so great about a town like Carcagente or any other small town in Spain. Here in Madrid, you can't go into any old house and say, "I think I'm going to stay for dinner 'cause I like the look of this place you got here," because the lady would call the police right away, because the lady from Madrid doesn't want a kid in her apartment unless he's the king's son or he's won a reality show.

The One-and-Only Susana was also gone for the summer. Her grandma took her on one of those senior citizen trips, because her mom, who's a regular citizen, can't stand her for a whole summer straight. I'm not surprised. I'm a junior citizen, and I had to put up with her for a whole school year, and I'm still paying for the terrible psychological consequences. Last week, I got a postcard from Susana with a picture of a beach somewhere in the Mediterranean on it. It said:

> Hi! Yesterday I got lost on this beach and all these old folks went looking for me. I found my way back by

myself but by then 10 old geezers had gone missing.
They showed up later that afternoon all sunburned
and starving. My grandma says they're going to kick
us out so I might see you soon.
Susana

Paquito Medina went to Vallecas for the summer. They
have an awesome city pool there, and his grandparents live
there, so in the afternoon they make him this milkshake
with cinnamon and lemon called *leche merengada*. Paquito
Medina's grandparents' house is a ton-a-cool: you open the
window, and you can see the Rayo Vallecano soccer stadium.
I know because Paquito Medina tells me about the view
fifty times a day. When I open the window in my apartment all I see is the Carabanchel jail, but I keep that to
myself about fifty times a day, because people tend to
respect you more if you live next to a stadium than if you
live next to a jail.

So, Our Nosy Neighbor Luisa has left us just like every
July, and she calls us every once in a while from Villa Luisa
to tell us that it's not hot at all in the sierra and to ask us
about her plants. Deep down, my mom's a good person:
not only does she water Luisa's plants, but she also opens
up all her drawers to make sure all of Luisa's things are still
in place.

Now we are the only inhabitants of a neighborhood
that looks like an abandoned planet, and that makes my

mom real nervous. First, she yells at us, and then she feels bad so she buys us ice creams. We're up to an average of five lectures and five ice creams a day.

Next month my grandpa might take us to Mota del Cuervo, his hometown. He has a house there with a few light bulbs on the ceiling and an outhouse. It's going to be just me, my grandpa, and the Bozo, so that my mom can take a break from us and so that she can go with the truck and my dad to a hotel where they make you breakfast and they make your bed.

Today I got a postcard from Ozzy—he's in Miranda de Ebro, this town that has a lot of postcards—and it says:

> Hey, Fore-eyes, I haven't thought about you, not even once. Since I don't got any friends here, I fight with my sister, who wears a retainer. Don't you get bored spending the whole summer in Carabanchel?
>
> A kick from your friend,
>
> Ozzy

I already wrote him back. Last year I didn't, and he made me pay for it. This is what I wrote:

> Hi Ozzy. Yeah, I get pretty bored, but there is one good thing—you're not here. I would like to tell the mayor of Miranda that it would be great if you stayed there forever. I know it's a dream that will never come true. It

hurts me that you write <u>four-eyes</u> like <u>fore-eyes</u>. I'm telling you in a letter because I know in person you would break my glasses. If you miss me, you should throw your sister's retainer on the ground—that way you'll feel like you're back in Hangman's Park throwing my glasses on the ground. My mom was wondering why it's been so long since I've broken my glasses. I told her it's because you're on vacation.

Don't come back,

Four-Eyes

As you can see, I'm a real tough guy in a letter, but in real life, things change a bit.

Summer in Carabanchel is like everywhere else in the world: there's a swimming pool, there's ice cream, there's *siesta* time, and there's a time when it's cool out. Me and my grandpa and the Bozo go down to Hangman's Park every afternoon, we buy a super-duper ice-cream cone, and we flop down on the bench until it gets dark and my grandpa says, "Your mom doesn't realize it, but there are times when we live like millionaires."

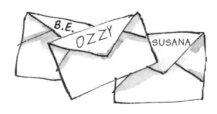

2

Luisa's Got a Lot of Nerve

Our Nosy Neighbor Luisa came back from her summer house in Miraflores de la Sierra just for the Reconciliation Dinner. The Reconciliation Dinner was in a Chinese restaurant that opened recently below our apartment. It's called Ching-Chong. They decided to call it that because the cook is from Chinchón, a small town just south of Madrid, and since the waiter is from China, they added the two g's on the end and the hyphen in the middle. Luisa keeps telling the Chinese waiter that he should marry the cook from Chinchón, because Luisa says that it isn't normal for a man and a woman to be partners without being married. When Luisa starts saying stuff like that, my grandpa just tells her, "You're the one who's not normal, Luisa."

Really, what's killing Our Nosy Neighbor Luisa is that she's curious about what their kids would be like, half from China, half from Chinchón. I know that because I heard her say it one Sunday after her third cocktail.

The Reconciliation Dinner was a success because the ones who had to reconcile were Luisa and my mom, and when we got to dessert they were toasting each other every three minutes. Not to criticize or anything, because I don't like that, but they'd had a couple bottles of wine—with the help of my dad and Bernabé, of course, who always help out when they can. So basically, they thought everything was funny. But I thought they were laughing too loud. The people at the next table were fed up with them laughing, and I was pretty embarrassed. I asked my mom three times to please lower her laugh and for them to stop pounding on the table, and the third time she went:

"Oh, son, leave me alone and let me laugh the way I want to," and then she said to Luisa, "See, he's driving me crazy lately. He won't stop telling me what to do: don't put that on, don't do that. He's a control freak. Reminds me of my mother."

That's how they repay me for being concerned about them. I think it's part of being a good kid, not wanting your parents to look stupid. My mom says it's more part of being a party pooper. I guess there are two different ways of looking at anything. Whatever.

I went over to look at the happy Buddha they had in the

back of the fish tank. Poor guy, so fat and nude with only the fish for friends. No one can be a happy Buddha in those conditions. I thought that the next time we came to Ching-Chong, I would bring a little Michelin Man keychain my dad gave me and put it next to Buddha. Buddha and the Michelin Man, two happy submarines. . . . The Bozo whacked me on the arm and brought me back to reality: he had two chopsticks stuck up his nose.

"Baby like Uncle Fester."

His favorite character is Uncle Fester from *The Addams Family*, and he likes to do all the silly things Fester does. This year he asked for Uncle Fester for his birthday. We felt pretty stupid going from toy store to toy store asking for a stuffed Uncle Fester. So, in the end, when we were tired of searching all around town, my mom bought him Nemo instead. I said to her, "He's not gonna like it, I'm telling you."

"Why won't he like it? Kids like all kinds of stuffed animals," she said.

I warned her. When he opened the package—so excited to have his own Uncle Fester—and saw Nemo, his eyes filled with tears. He put his pacifier in his mouth and put Nemo up on the minibar, and that's where it's been ever since. You can't pull something like that and expect the Bozo not to notice.

But getting back to the famous Reconciliation Dinner: my mom and Luisa were toasting each other and laughing up a storm, my dad and Bernabé started singing, my grandpa wouldn't stop asking the waiter what the secret to Chinese food was, and the Bozo had chopsticks up his nose. (Every once in a while he'd take the chopsticks out and find a little green present, and then he'd put them back in. For him, everything is recyclable.) I felt like the only normal member of The Addams Family, which from now on we can refer to as the García Moreno Family. Man, they could make a killer movie about us! In Hollywood, they don't know what they're missing here in Carabanchel.

At this point in this exciting chapter, you are probably wondering why these two great friends called Luisa and Cata (a.k.a. my mom) were mad at each other.

I will start this intense story as usual, from the beginning of time. . . .

So, like every summer, Luisa went away to her mansion, which is a pretty impressive one. Luisa says tourists stop to see it, especially at night, when all the dwarfs in the yard are lit up. Instead of real lights, she put out dwarfs that light up on the lawn. There are also fences made of millstones painted green. And the house is the shape of a little castle. One of the towers is the chimney. The people in Miraflores call it "the witch's house." They must've gotten the character wrong, because Luisa built the house with Snow White in mind, not the witch. And Snow White was the one who lived with the dwarfs; that's common knowledge. But people don't pay attention to these details. So no matter how peeved Luisa gets, in all of Miraflores, her house is known as "the witch's house."

The afternoon before Luisa and Bernabé left, Luisa came up to our apartment and asked my mom if she could do her a favor and water her plants, and my mom said, "That's what neighbors are for."

Shortly after, Luisa came back up and said to my mom: "Hey, hon, since you're going to be taking care of my plants, would you mind shutting and opening my blinds three times a day?"

What happened was that Luisa saw this report on the news about all the things you should do to make sure you're not robbed when you're away for the summer. And my mom said that she'd do it for her, as a neighbor and a friend. Then Luisa came up a third time to add:

"When you go down at night to open my blinds, could you also turn the lights on and then after an hour turn them back off, 'cause that's another thing the police department said to do. That way the thieves will think we're having dinner at home."

And my mom said, "Well, sure."

"And can you get my mail, too, 'cause when they see the mailbox's full, they know the people are on vacation. That's not too much to ask, is it?"

And my mom said, "Of course."

But as soon as Luisa left, my mom said something slightly different. She said, "Man, that Luisa's got a lot of nerve. She takes advantage of the fact that I'm the only one who's stuck here while everyone else is on vacation, and on top of it all I have to take care of the neighbors' apartments. And then nobody even thanks me for it, and Luisa is the worst about that. Would it hurt her to say, 'I'll take Manolito for a few days, and he can go swimming in the pool at Miraflores.'"

These are the things my mom was thinking out loud—actually, screaming real loud (my mom shouts as she thinks)—when the doorbell rang for the fourth time. Who was it? You guessed it: good ol' Luisa, the one with the same nerve as before. What did she want? Here you have it:

"Look, Cata, I thought about Manolito, the poor guy, here all summer without an ounce of fun or any friends, not even bad ones . . ."

As she was saying this, my mom already had one foot in the closet to pack my backpack. But my mom stopped dead in her tracks, because Luisa finished her sentence:

". . . so I thought I'd give him my canary and the fish tank, so the little guy can have some fun."

My mom stood there with her jaw wide open. Ten minutes later, we had the canary's cage and the fish tank on top of the minibar. Luisa didn't give us Miss Bonnie because, ever since she found out that the Bozo lets Miss Bonnie use his pacifier, she's scared that my brother's going to give her dog some kind of disease. I understand her concern.

My mother talked to herself in the kitchen for at least half an hour while she made dinner. She talked about her sad life, about the summer she was going to spend looking after Our Nosy Neighbor Luisa's apartment (while my dad was out on Spain's highways), and having to take care of my grandpa, the Bozo (who still cannot control his bodily functions), some strange fish and canary, and me (who she says makes her head spin with all my talking). That made the rest of us feel bad, of course, because we're not made of stone, you know. My grandpa came in the kitchen and began making himself some dinner.

"What are you doing, Dad?" my mom asked him.

"Getting ready to eat. I don't need to be taken care of by

anyone. I don't want to be a bother."

Then I came in, and I didn't open my mouth the whole time. Since I didn't talk, neither did the Bozo. I already told you: I'm his leader.

"And what's wrong with *you* now?" my mom asked me.

"I don't want to be a bother, either," I answered her, like a poor little offended kid.

But we had to forgive her right away, because my mom is so weird that she likes it better when you do the exact thing she's complaining about. And if you don't forgive her immediately, she starts crying (she's just like the Bozo that way). So we always follow the advice my dad gives us on Mondays before he gets in his truck:

"Do what she wants, and you will be happy."

The next day we went down to Luisa's apartment to follow all of the police department's instructions. My mom found the cartoons that Luisa taped off the TV for us with her VCR (Luisa is a little behind the times with these things), so that once a month we'll let them wax their legs in peace (and the Bozo isn't tempted to stick his pacifier in the wax). Following the same logic, my mom thought that she could put a tape on for us every afternoon while Luisa was gone, and she could go up to our apartment and take a nap in peace.

"I should get paid in some way for what I'm doing for her," my mom said during one of her noisy thoughts.

Anyway, the Bozo and I began going down to Luisa's to watch cartoons while my grandpa and my mom snored in unison upstairs. We'd take off our shoes, we'd have a deadly cheese fight, and then we'd lay down to watch cartoons. Since there were only two or three cartoons, after a week we knew them all by heart, and I could fall asleep halfway through and then wake up right before the end. I highly recommend this experience. You only need: a couch, a VCR, and a cartoon you've seen fifty times. A cartoon you know down to every last detail gives you a lot of freedom: you can get up to go to the bathroom, fall asleep, get into a fight with your best friend. As long as you see the beginning and the end, you're good. The endings are always much more exciting, and there are times when they make you cry even if the cartoon is a bore galore (they're tears of happiness, in that case).

So, yeah, I was saying that I fell asleep, without realizing that the Bozo, who we can consider a disciple of the Tasmanian Devil, stayed awake and had a whole hour of freedom to do his own thing. He's the type of kid who could use a security guard assigned to him 24/7. While I was sleeping, the Bozo took the tape out of the VCR and put two of his *Star Wars* action figures, Chewbacca and C-3PO, in the opening. Then, he woke me up Bozo-style, with his unmistakable slaps in the face.

"What's your problem, man?" I asked him, my heart racing at 350 beats per second.

"Baby wanna watch *Star Wars*, see Chewie and C-3P on TV."

"Well, Baby's gonna have to suck it up because we don't have *Star Wars* on tape."

"Yes, we do. Baby put them in." He pointed to the player.

"What have you done, you little monster?" I didn't call him monster to insult him; I called him that because he deserved it.

I tried to stick my hand in the opening, but I couldn't reach back far enough. And I didn't want to stick it back too far. Ever since we were little, my mom's warned us about being electrocuted to death.

All of a sudden, that very same mother I am always telling you about opened the door. When she saw me with my hand in Luisa's VCR, her eyes bulged out.

"What are you doing, you little monster?"

As you can see, the term "monster" is quite common in my family. We use it with each other whenever we get the chance; of course, we're all careful to use it only with someone below us in age and rank.

"Baby wanna watch Chewie and C-3P on TV." The Bozo was not backing down from his plan.

"He stuck them in here, and I can't get them out," I explained.

"And you let him?" my mom asked.

"I didn't realize he was doing it. . . . I fell asleep."

"Don't you know that you can't fall asleep with this kid around?"

I wanted to say to her, "Well, that doesn't stop you from taking a nap," but I didn't because I love life and I know those kinds of comments make her pretty furious.

My sweet mother went to yank my hand out of the VCR, but she couldn't because my hand was now nice and stuck. Don't ask me how a hand that was able to go in can't come back out again. My body was overcome with fear, and I started sweating. The thought of spending the rest of my life with my hand stuck in Luisa's VCR was pretty frightening. Unless . . . they cut my hand off! Then I thought about how every time I would come down to Luisa's and see the VCR, I'd think, "Aw, my poor hand's in there." Then my body was overcome with fear all over again. I thought about how I could get electrocuted and with a very weak voice, I said to my mom, "Please unplug it."

My mom unplugged it. You gotta give her that; it was a humane gesture. But the only thing she was worried about was the cost of repairing Luisa's VCR if we broke it (especially since it's so ancient). Obviously, having a son with only one hand was of secondary importance to her.

She went to the bathroom and came back with her hands all soapy. Then she rubbed my hand with hers until finally my hand slid out. My mom dried the VCR, took us both by the hands, and said, "Nothing happened here. Whoever tells Luisa about this gets his tongue cut off."

I'm always left wondering if my mom is totally serious when she says that kind of stuff or if she's only half serious.

A few days later, Luisa came home because she wanted to make sure we were following her instructions. When she tried to put a tape in, the VCR didn't work and she called a repairman. The repairman extracted one Chewbacca and one C-3PO from inside the player, and when he saw the soap residue, he said to Luisa:

"You don't need to clean the inside of the VCR, lady; just dusting off the outside is plenty."

Luisa stormed up to our apartment. She threw Chewbacca and C-3PO on the table and yelled at my mom, "So I ask you to protect my apartment from robbers, and you guys sneak in there yourselves!"

I thought my mom was going to yell back at her, but, once again, she surprised us. My mom grabbed the fish tank and put it in Luisa's arms, then she gave her the canary's cage, and when Luisa was balancing the fish tank and the cage in both arms, my mom said to her in an alarmingly calm voice, "There, you have your little animals. The next time you go away, your mother can follow your little police department instructions."

Luisa left real angry but real slowly, because she didn't want to spill the fish tank water. Leaving real angry with a fish tank and a canary's cage in your hands has got to be pretty tough.

The big fight between my mom and Luisa went on for a week. That whole week they didn't speak a word to each other. We were two enemy families, because even though my godfather never gets mad, Luisa forbade Bernabé to talk to us, and my mom did the same thing with my dad.

I asked my grandpa if he thought Bernabé was going to change his will and leave everything to some other kid. (I've told you before that the Bozo and I are his only heirs on this planet, right?)

"Not unless Luisa makes him, but I don't think so," my grandpa answered.

As soon as he mentioned her name, the doorbell rang.

"I can't live without you, my babies, my Cata, my grandpa Nicolás. . . . You're my real family." Our Nosy Neighbor Luisa took out a handkerchief from her sleeve and wiped away a tear that none of us really saw. She must have wiped it away before it came out of her eye. "Nothing is more silly than getting mad over a video. Cata, I want you to accept a Reconciliation Dinner next week."

My mom wiped away her own invisible tear and said, "We'll be there."

When Luisa left, my mom changed to her police inspector face and thought out loud, "I wonder what she wants me to do this time?"

She had the answer a second later because Luisa rang the doorbell again. I, personally, think she was behind the door the whole time. Luisa, with her apartment keys in her hand, said, "Cata, if you don't mind . . ."

My mom took the keys from Luisa before she could finish. "Bring up the creatures whenever you want."

She's my mom, but she's real smart.

"The kids," said Luisa, "can watch cartoons whenever they want."

My mom went into the kitchen for a second, and Luisa

came over to us and, grabbing us by the arms, said in a terrifying voice, "Whoever puts another Chewbacca and C-3PO in my VCR is going to be sorry."

When my mom came back, Luisa explained to her what she had suggested to us: "I was telling them to be real careful with the VCR."

As you can see, there are many different ways of saying the same thing.

A week later, Luisa and Bernabé came from Miraflores for the great Reconciliation Dinner and, like I said before, my mom and Luisa were close again, the rest of us were singing, and the Bozo was doing his imitations of Uncle Fester. In other words, it was a huge success.

Afterward, Luisa and my godfather went back to Miraflores, and we went back to protecting their apartment from possible criminals. The Bozo and I also went back to spending naptime at Luisa's apartment. We know that if we break her VCR again, she's not going to be happy, but we don't care, and not because we're brave or anything, because we're not, but because even though my mom thinks we're going down to watch cartoons, we don't use the VCR anymore. We've found another treasure even more valuable: Luisa's bedroom. In her closet full of mirrors, she keeps all of Bernabé's toupees. She has them on top of mannequin heads, and the Bozo and I spend a lot of time brushing them and trying them on.

We also found Luisa's jewelry box. We pretend we're

pirates and that we've found a chest in a cave, and we put on all her necklaces and we take out Luisa's mink coats and we put them on, because we're pirates in the North Sea. The first day I put Luisa's rabbit hair coat on the Bozo, the Bozo fell off the bed from the weight of the coat. Man, that was scary! He just lay there on the ground, not moving, covered by the coat. He likes to play those kinds of tricks on me. I told you he's a pretty dismal child.

When we get tired of pretending to be pirates, we lie down on Luisa and Bernabé's bed and, just like that, with the toupees, the jewelry, and the coats, we take a nap. I guess we have a lot of nerve. Since I know that the Bozo pees in the bed every time he goes to sleep, whether it's at nighttime or in the afternoon, I put one of the coats under him and I can sleep easy, because I know that between now and the winter, when Luisa goes to put on her minks, the Bozo's super-pee will have dried.

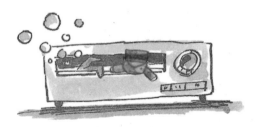

3

Life or Death

Yesterday I was checking out my new bathing suit in my mom's mirror, and I thought:

"I'm a whole lotta cool."

I admit it'd be kind of a weird thing to say out loud, unless you're cocky like Ozzy the Bully, but I'm sure a lot of people think it. The lifeguard at the Carabanchel pool thinks it: he's so conceited, every so often I see him looking at his super biceps, and I just know he's thinking, "I'm a whole lotta cool." Bernabé thinks it when he brushes his toupee with a wet comb on Sunday morning and looks at himself in the hallway mirror before going out. I see him smile and think, "I'm a whole lotta cool." My grandpa thinks it when he puts on his Ninja Turtle sweatsuit and goes down to buy bread, and the baker says to him, "That

Ninja Turtle sweatsuit looks great on you. You look fifty years younger."

I would bet my piggy bank that at that precise moment, my grandpa is thinking, "I'm a whole lotta cool."

The One-and-Only Susana thinks it when she walks by the bench in Hangman's Park where Ozzy, Big Ears, and I are sitting. We stop insulting each other and stop being bored for a minute to look at her while she walks past without asking us the time of day. I'm convinced that inside her enigmatic mind there is a five word sentence: "I'm a whole lotta cool."

So it's really no surprise that when I saw myself in that bathing suit with wild palm trees on it, I took a deep breath, pounded my fists on my chest three times and, after coughing for a while (I had pounded kinda hard), I thought the same thing as all those people I just mentioned. I'm human, too, you know.

I let out a yell that would've deafened even Tarzan's monkey, while I thought to myself with all my might: "I'm a whole lotta cooooooooooooooooooool!"

We were going to the pool, but that wasn't the best part: we were going to the pool *without* my mom. I love my mom to deadly death, but at the pool we have different strategies. She doesn't like it when we gargle in the water, when we do aquatic farts, when we splash her, when we do cannonballs, or when we pretend to be poor drowning kids as we doggy paddle by her. She doesn't understand those kinds of jokes.

I don't like it when she smears me with sunscreen every five minutes, when she makes me wait two hours after lunch before I can go in the pool, and when she makes me get dressed in the women's locker room so she can keep an eye on me. You gotta admit, it's kind of embarrassing. You're in R-rated situations. The girls get undressed in front of you, and then they get upset if you look at those parts of the human body where your eyes automatically go. One girl last year said to me, "Hey, squirt, quit staring. You haven't blinked in about five minutes."

I just don't understand that kind of reaction, I swear.

Thank goodness, this time my grandpa was going to take us, because even though he's said on various occasions that he'd like to change in the women's locker room, he settles for the men's.

We had planned to meet Big Ears at the pool entrance. It was going to be a totally awesome day. It was going to be a day I was going to remember for the rest of my life, for sure.

To be honest, it took us a long time to get going, because my mom insisted on emptying the contents of the refrigerator into our backpacks. She was going for the tenth yogurt when my grandpa got between her and the backpack and yelled, "Catalina, for God's sake, we're not going to climb Mount Everest!"

My mom, who never gives up, got busy with other preparations: she put SPF thirty sunblock in my backpack for the Bozo, plus shovels and pails, a raft, two bathing suits to change into, two bathrobes, some Band-Aids, and ointment in case we stepped on a broken beer bottle some thugs just broke. She always prepares for the worst. That's how I am, too, totally a worrywart. Sometimes I ask myself what talk-show program on TV I'd like to be on if some terrible tragedy ever happened to me. Our Teach, Miss Asunción, says that my brain is rotting from all the horrible atrocities I see on TV. But she's wrong. For me it's enough to hear about all the horrible atrocities my mom imagines. I mean, they should hire her in Hollywood to write the thirteenth sequel to *Friday the 13th*.

She gave us twenty-five kisses in person and blew us another twenty-five from the window. We thought we were free of her until my grandpa's cell phone rang. He's got a special ring tone for my mom: the theme from *Jaws*. So we knew it was her. She just wanted to remind us to put sunscreen on the Bozo and to wet his head and to put his baseball cap on and to please not drown, because that would be very unpleasant. For once, we were in agreement.

Our totally awesome day wasn't starting out so great. My grandpa got mad at the guard at the pool entrance because Mr. Guard Man said my grandpa couldn't come in unless he changed into a bathing suit, and my grandpa said he'd rather die than make a fool of himself. Believe it or not, my grandpa has never worn a bathing suit in his life, and his stomach looks like it's been bleached with Clorox. Mr. Guard Man was set on making my grandpa strip down, and my grandpa said to him, "I don't get it. Why do you want to see an old guy naked? Just ask my grandson. He'll tell you: it's not worth it."

I told Mr. Guard Man that it was true: my grandpa nude is nothing great.

They were finally able to come up with a compromise: my grandpa agreed to switch his beret for the Bozo's SpongeBob baseball cap.

The guard said, "There, that's much better. Now you're presentable."

Pool guards have very strange taste.

At last, they let us in.

My grandpa sat on a bench, took out his false teeth (see, he gets undressed!), and after five minutes he was totally out, his mouth wide open and his head tilted up to the sun. He's just like a sunflower.

Big Ears and I put red plastic sunglasses on him, and we left him snoring behind us.

We let the Bozo go in the kiddie pool with all his shovels and his fifty buckets, and we went to act out some mortal drownings in the big-people pool.

Man, did we have a whole lotta fun! We were about to drown a few times for real because we were laughing so hard. We'd get on each other's shoulders and end up tipping over. You know, those kinds of sidesplitting things that my mom doesn't find the least bit funny.

We did a ton of belly flops. It's pretty painful, but there are worse things in life: going to school, for example. Plus, in my neighborhood almost all the kids do belly flops and nobody complains out loud. Only sometimes we grab our stomachs with a look of terrible pain on our faces. We're tough people.

Big Ears dove in so hard that blood came out of his nose. Big Ears has blood coming out of his nose every day, from one thing or another. Miss Espe, the school therapist, says it's psychological, but c'mon, I can testify that on this occasion it was not psychological; it was because Big Ears did such a huge belly flop that he almost emptied all the water out of the pool.

So much blood was coming out of his nose that we both thought the best thing he could do was stay in the pool and let the water clean him off, since chlorine has healing powers.

A minute later, two ladies with a lifeguard were trying to get us kicked out. One of them was so mad that she grabbed the lifeguard's whistle to threaten us. What a scene! The ladies were saying how gross it was and where were our mothers to teach us some manners. Sometimes ladies aren't humane. They think blood in movies is sad and moving, but real blood is gross. One of them put a cotton ball in Big Ears' nose, and she put it in so far you could almost see it coming out of his eye. On top of everything, I had to thank them. Me, of course. Big Ears doesn't have any manners: what he's got is a lot of nerve.

When the hemorrhaging stopped, we went back to the crime scene—the pool—and for a good while, we had a sick crocodile fight (a super-realistic fight, you could bite and everything). In that kind of game, we get mad real easy. It's hard to control yourself when you're taking bites out of your enemy, so we sat down on the steps. Big Ears checked his fantastic underwater watch: it had been half an hour since we started the crocodile fight and an hour since we left my grandpa out like a light.

Our fingers looked like prunes. We decided that crucial moment had arrived when your grandpa gives you money for an ice cream.

On our way back to my grandpa, we saw a group of ladies (including the two from before) huddled around a kid lying on his back with twenty-five shovels in his hand. The kid was beet-red like one of those crabs that my mom likes to eat so much.

The red kid was my brother.

I started to cry right away. I was crying because my brother was so red and because one of the ladies was yelling at my grandpa, saying he was an irresponsible grandpa. The lifeguard with the super biceps picked up my brother to put him in a cab so we could take him to the hospital. My grandpa and I were crying as we followed the lifeguard. It looked like a funeral. So many tears were coming out that I couldn't see anything out of my glasses. The ladies were saying that the Bozo had symptoms of first-degree sunstroke. That had to be something awful.

When we got to the hospital, I called my mom. To calm her down, I told her, "Don't worry. It's a life or death

matter. Come right away. There's no time to waste."

I heard a bloodcurdling scream on the other end and then silence. My grandpa, with his prostate problems and all the stress, had to go to the bathroom. The lady nurse asked me what I was to the Bozo, and I told her I was his brother. The lady nurse asked me what the Bozo's name was, and I started to cry again and told her I couldn't remember. Then my grandpa came back and said a historic sentence:

"The child's name is Nicolás García Moreno."

So my brother's name was Nicolás, like my grandpa. Not the Bozo. How nice. In the future, I'd have to get used to calling him by his name.

A little while later, my mom got there. She didn't look like herself: she was all white like EVE in *WALL·E*. Our Nosy Neighbor Luisa had driven her to the hospital. My mom didn't look at my grandpa or me. She went directly to see my brother. When she came out, she said the Bozo was going to spend the night there. Me and my grandpa started crying again. And while we were crying, my mom and Luisa yelled at us. They told my grandpa he was an irresponsible grandpa and they told me I was very mean, that I didn't put SPF thirty on my brother, that I hadn't put his cap on him (What was I going to do? My grandpa was wearing it.), and that I didn't take care of him because I don't love him. Now *that* wasn't true. I'll swear it with my hand on the Bible before the president of Spain if necessary.

That night's dinner was the saddest one of our lives. We couldn't stop thinking about the Bozo, with those big white undies they put on him in the hospital. I'm sure he peed in his bed half the night. My mom said that this way we would learn to love my brother more. Since she was so sad, she bought me a super-ice-cream cone for dessert. I ate it, yes I did, but between tears. I ate it to comfort myself, and it actually worked.

I got into bed without taking a bath, because a bath without the Bozo and our spectacular water fart championship just isn't a bath.

The next day, Luisa and my mom went to pick up the Bozo. Me and my grandpa waited by the door the whole time. An hour later we saw Luisa's car pull up (it stalled three times before they reached our building).

The Bozo got out of the car with his hands loaded: he still had his shovels, buckets, and some rubber balls they bought him. He wasn't so red anymore. The Bozo didn't hold a grudge against us because he still doesn't know what a grudge is, and it was neat having him with us again. When night came we couldn't have our famous water fart championship in the bathtub on account of him still recovering, but they let him sleep with me and Grandpa on the sofa bed. I didn't care if he wet it. He slept holding his pacifier in his hand. I think he was scared some unscrupulous person would steal it.

It's not true that I don't love my brother, just that I forgot to put SPF thirty on him. I get distracted sometimes.

By the way, I forget: what is his name again?

4

Archimedes'
Principle

The García Moreno Principle

I'm a kid of principle. You gotta believe me. I'm not like Ozzy, who's all cocky and who would stab you in the back just to get ahead. I know you shouldn't laugh if an old person falls down, that you shouldn't make fun of people who wear toupees, that you shouldn't take advantage of clumsy people (if you wanna know the truth, that's not a problem, since I'm the clumsiest of them all). But, anyway, these are principles that I find difficult to follow sometimes because, to be honest, when an old person falls down, the most natural thing is to fall on the ground, too, laughing. Thank goodness that when that happens, my principles immediately go to work: a grandpa falls down, I bite my lip with all my superhuman might, and I'm telling you, that laugh turns into a cry real fast.

One time my glasses witnessed my dear old grandfather and his best friend, Mr. Faustino, roll down a whole flight of stairs in my building. They were falling all over each other as they went down. Parts of their bodies kept coming loose: my grandpa's dentures went flying, as if he had let out a terrifying scream, and Mr. Faustino's cane did a perfect curve in the air like a javelin. I realized I was about to toss my principles out the window, and I bit my lower lip so hard it almost came off, I'm not kidding. "I can afford to lose my lower lip, but I won't lose my principles," I thought while I was crouched on all fours looking for my grandpa's dentures.

A kid of principle, that's what I am. But there are some principles I won't follow. Why? Because Mother Nature won't let me. One of them is Archimedes' Principle.

Our Nosy Neighbor Luisa read me Archimedes' Principle one day before my swimming classes began. Luisa told my mom that doing sports was a good way of ensuring that I didn't wind up a hooligan. In the pool, the hooligans are the ones who just fool around the whole time; you know, like having aquatic burping and underwater gargling contests. I thought, "Well, that's what I am: a pool hooligan," because Big Ears and I, we spend the whole time in the water doing gross things that I won't tell you about because you'll probably lose your lunch.

Luisa said that nowadays everyone who is anyone is an expert at some sport: golf, skiing, sailing, horse racing. . . . But in Carabanchel we don't have the ocean or mountains or a racetrack. Instead of golf, we have bocce—that's a type of golf with no grass, and no clubs and no greens and no holes. (Not to brag or anything, but my grandpa is the super-champion of the Hangman's Park Bocce Cup.)

Instead of skiing, we have some cardboard cartons we use to slide down the Gully, which is this dirt slope behind my apartment building. When you're almost to the bottom of the Gully, it's better if you close your eyes: the end of the race consists of smashing into some old washing machines that were left there back in the day. But don't go getting any ideas; the washing machines don't work. If they worked, we would've taken them a long time ago, don't you think?

As far as the racetrack is concerned, since we don't have any horses, we make do with Ozzy, who's a mule. He's very good at what he does. He only has two legs but with the way he acts, you'd think he had four. When it comes time to kick people and things, no one's better than Ozzy.

So, anyway, my mom and Our Nosy Neighbor Luisa got together and signed me up for swimming lessons at the neighborhood pool. Luisa said that having a healthy body would help me have a healthy mind (and not the dirty mind everyone who's read my books says I have).

I tried telling her that it went against my principles to get into a pool that was too deep to stand in—unless the metal ladder is nearby and I'm with Big Ears, who is just as useless as I am when it comes to swimming. It's not that I hate the water. I love water. But what's the point of swimming across it? Riddle me that. Didn't it occur to those two women that they were sending me to my death? I'm not kidding here, *amigos*. I know those lifeguard instructors at our neighborhood pool: they love to sit back and count the last few bubbles of poor defenseless kids who end up at the bottom of the pool.

But Luisa always gets her way, so she brought out the encyclopedia she bought a few years back so she'd be ready in case they called her from *Who Wants to Be a Millionaire?* (or from some other intellectual game show) to be a phone-a-friend lifeline. Then she read in a professor-like voice the famous Principle of Archimedes:

"Any body immersed in a fluid is buoyed up by a force equal to the weight of the displaced fluid."

We all just sat there without saying a word. On the one hand, we were impressed; on the other hand, we hadn't understood a word of it. Luisa, looking at us like we were all a bunch of idiots, explained, "Manolito, you're going to float like any other body. Archimedes said so back in his day, and I'm saying so now."

"And even if he doesn't float, I don't care. He's going to learn to swim like a real person!" my mom added. "I tell you, if it's not one thing, it's another. He's always finding stuff wrong with everything. How many times have I seen this kid playing in the pool with his friend?"

A typical mother, willing to risk the life of her child just to save face with a neighbor.

"Yeah, knowing all those fancy strokes is really going to

come in handy here in Carabanchel," said my grandpa. But my mom and Luisa didn't even look at him. In my apartment, my grandpa has no say in anything. He's just like me.

No one could save me from my own awful fate.

A few days later I found myself on the edge of an Olympic-sized swimming pool, praying that Archimedes' little principle didn't fail him (or me) while trying to follow the lesson on arm movement that the super-lifeguard was giving us. I looked at his arm, then at mine, and thought how unfair the world was. Up until recently, I believed that story about the ugly duckling, who everyone looked down on and then one fine day, out of the blue, he turned into a spectacular swan. But I realized that in real life things don't always turn out so amazing: I saw some pictures of my dad when he was little, and he was just like me, short and scrawny, so I think I'll be just like him when I grow up. Instead of having muscle in our upper arms, we García Morenos prefer to have it around our waist. It's our body type; that's all there is to it. Luisa and my mom didn't want to miss out on that historic day when I would become an Olympic swimmer. They were on the side of the pool, all proud and clapping real loud every time I did the arm movements. I was pumping my arms, imagining I was doing the breaststroke across the North Atlantic. I was getting very excited. Olympic swimming was fun! But then, Super-muscles yelled, "Now the same thing, but in the water!"

All the kids jumped in without thinking twice. I thought about it twice, three times, then four. I just stood there. Suddenly, the thought of being in there with ten feet of water under me made me feel light-headed. My mom and Luisa watched me with anxious looks on their faces. Luisa's look said, "Remember Archimedes." My mom's look said, "Son, why do you always have to be different from the rest of humanity?"

Super-muscles looked down at me; no, I mean, really looked down at me (he was about five feet taller than me) and said in a puzzled voice, "García Moreno, what are you waiting for?"

García Moreno (that's me) dove in, at last, because of all the mental pressure that was being placed upon him. And García Moreno noticed that his body was falling—*splat*—into liquid, and no matter how hard Archimedes tried, García Moreno's body did not float up to the top but instead kept going down and down and down.

García Moreno remembers only that he cried tears of relief when he finally took a breath at the edge of the pool. His mother—well, my mother—was hugging him. Her clothes were totally soaked. She had saved me from a humiliating public death. And that's saying a lot, because my mom is another one who doesn't stray far from the metal ladder. But she has the makings of a hero.

The lifeguard said that having my mom and Our Nosy Neighbor Luisa at the first lesson was "counterproductive," that they shouldn't spoil me so much, and that I was never going to become a man. I wished really hard that someday Archimedes' Principle wouldn't work for that beast of a human being, either. Super-biceps obviously didn't have any feelings, and that's exactly what Luisa said to his face:

"Let's pray that this little guy never turns into a man like you."

Luisa was on my side! I felt sorry for the instructor, because no matter how strong an instructor is, getting in a fight with Our Nosy Neighbor Luisa is a lost cause.

In a very meek voice, I asked to have my glasses back. If, at a moment like that, when you're about to kick the bucket, you're nearsighted and on top of it all you can't find your glasses, the worldwide world becomes an awful place. When you've been on death's doorstep, like I have, you think long and hard about what you want your last wish to be: mine is that, no matter how horrible the circumstances, I want to die wearing my glasses.

I don't even want to think about what would happen if I entered the other world and left my glasses behind in this one. There has never been a case, at least that I am aware of, in which a dead person has gone back home because they forgot their glasses. I'm not the only one in my family with a strange request like that: my grandpa, for example, keeps telling us over and over that we better not bury him without his brand-new dentures.

When I got home, Luisa and my mom comforted and pampered me. They didn't seem to care that I would never become a man and that I'd spend my whole life being a kid who doggy paddles. They said they'd never seen a body sink so fast in a liquid before.

That afternoon, Ozzy came up with one of his typical wise-guy explanations of what happened to me. Ozzy said

I sank because I have rocks in my head. Everyone in our gang laughed. As usual they were sucking up to him. Traitors!

According to my dad, Archimedes' Principle doesn't apply to any body whose last name is García Moreno. A body named García Moreno that is submersed in a liquid . . . disappears. Word of this strange occurrence has spread, and scientists from all over the world are on their way right now to Carabanchel to meet in person this extraordinary kid who, single-handedly, shattered such an ancient principle.

That extraordinary kid is none other than . . . me, Manolito Four-Eyes!

García Moreno Principle

5

Nicolás Timberlake

If my grandpa had major plastic surgery, and they made his face all soft and smooth like the Bozo's behind, I would still be able to spot him in a lineup of a thousand people, because no matter how hard he tries to hide, there's a test you can do to pick my grandpa out from the rest of the inhabitants of planet Earth. This test is much more reliable than a secret birthmark or wart (both of which he has).

Here's how to run the test: You stand in front of a line of people a mile long, you put on a CD with some *paso doble* music (that's the music they play at bullfights in Spain), and then you sit back and wait eagerly for the results. There will always be one guy who will break

53

formation, who will dance out of line with a big smile on his face and his arms up like he has them around a big, strong, invisible woman. That guy is, without a question of a doubt, Nicolás Moreno, my grandpa. He knows it, and he's not ashamed to admit it in public:

"Whenever I hear a *paso doble,* my feet start a-movin' and I can't control them."

Where there's an orchestra, there's my grandpa. Sometimes on Sunday mornings he sneaks out with the Bozo. He doesn't say where he's going. My mom, who must be a distant relative of James Bond, says, "There goes your grandpa to look for the goat people."

The goat people are a couple of guys who go down to Hangman's Park with an accordion and a goat and play *paso doble* music. My mom and I will look out the window and see my grandpa holding the Bozo and dancing whatever they throw at him. My mom says, "This guy is a piece of work. Does he know how silly he looks?"

But my dad sticks up for my grandpa. "Would you leave him alone? Let him dance all he wants."

One time my mom, who always says whatever's on her mind, leaned out the window really far, till her feet were off the floor, and yelled, "For God's sake, Dad, you're embarrassing our family!"

"I'm embarrassing *you?* Cata, the whole neighborhood can hear you."

"Good for the neighborhood. I don't care. *Daaaaaad!*"

But my grandpa was so excited about his *paso doble*

that he didn't hear her anymore. Only the Bozo realized that everyone was staring down at them from their apartments, and each time my grandpa twirled the Bozo around, he'd hold up his pacifier to wave at them. My mom yelled again, but it didn't do any good. I noticed that every time she screamed her legs got a little farther off the ground, but since she doesn't like it when I interrupt while she's doing something, I kept my mouth shut. And that's how I almost lost my mom. All of a sudden she let out a hair-raising shriek, and my dad jumped up from the sofa and grabbed her by the ankles. My mom sat down on the floor and cried, because she was so shaken up.

"Catalina, if you make another scene like this, you're going to fall out the window and I'm going to die of a heart attack," my dad said.

Not a very pleasant thought, losing both your parents at the same time, before your very own eyes. And they're always saying I have nightmares because I watch violent stuff on TV. Ha! My apartment is way scarier than any TV show.

You're probably thinking that after this terrible incident, my mom learned her lesson and has stopped yelling out the window at my grandpa. You're wrong. She still yells at him, but before she does, she takes some precautions. She says to my dad, "Manolo, grab on to my skirt, will you?"

So, my dad and I hold on to her skirt while she yells out the window.

"Why are you looking at me like that, Manolito? I'd rather look like a fool than have her kill us both," says my dad.

Well, I gotta admit, I agree with him.

My dad is a fan of letting people live their lives, and my mom is the opposite. On top of that, she's embarrassed that people have started calling my grandpa "Nicolás Timberlake" because he's an awesome dancer. Me, on the other hand, I'm super proud. I think it's a whole lotta cool. As you can see, in the García Moreno home, disagreement is the name of the game.

I've given you all this information so that you will understand why, on St. Peter's Day, which is a huge holiday in Carabanchel, my grandpa, the Bozo, and I were down in Hangman's Park two hours before the Great Paradise Orchestra got there—just because my grandpa wanted to watch while they set up the stage. He loves seeing how the singer gets in the truck to change and comes out all transformed, wearing one of those dresses that sparkle to the beat of the music.

My mom had told my grandpa to have us home by ten.

"Don't forget: ten o'clock!"

"You don't trust me, Catalina?"

"No!"

That's my mom for you: she always tells the truth no matter how painful it is.

But we weren't going to let anyone rain on our parade. After all, St. Peter's Day comes only once a year. The owners of Stumbles Bar had put up a food stand outside with some tables and stools. We were the first ones in line. My grandpa said, "The usual for me, and Coke for these two."

"These two" were me and the Bozo. Man, do I have to explain everything? Those were the first, but certainly not the last, Cokes of the night.

By the time the Great Paradise Orchestra started playing, my grandpa had bought us each at least two more Cokes. He doesn't like to drink alone. The Bozo and I had so much gas in our stomachs that we could've held five burping contests. I don't like to admit it, but when it comes to the art of burping, the Bozo is *número uno*. I'll never forget something my grandpa told me once: "You have to learn to be a good loser in life. The García Morenos are experts at that."

The first ones in all of Carabanchel on the dance floor were my grandpa, me, and the Bozo. I did it partly for the singer: it's sad when no one dances to the song you're singing. Luckily, by the third song other people started to dance, and I could go back to my place at the food stand and keep drinking Coke with Big Ears, who was sitting on one of the stools. Every once in a while, my grandpa and the Bozo would leave the dance floor and come over to have more Coke and "the usual." I don't know how many trips they made. There are some versions of the story that say ten—others, twelve. And the Bozo isn't even allowed to have Coke! My mom and his team of pediatricians have

strictly forbidden it, because he gets crazy-hyper, and we have to tie him to the bars of his crib so he's forced to lie down and go to sleep.

Hey, what I just said about tying him to the crib? It's not true. I hope you don't believe it and report us to the police.

You could say that my grandpa and the Bozo were the life of the party. Big Ears and I watched from our stools: now they were dancing to a Beatles song, now a rumba, then *"La Bamba."* Sometimes the Bozo would jump up and down, and other times he would lift his arms so that whoever was closest to him would pick him up, and they'd pass him from one person to the next and throw him up in the air. That's what he likes: being in the spotlight. But no one, not even the Bozo, can steal the stage from Nicolás Timberlake when he's on a roll—and that night he was on a roll.

What happened next is still being talked about in Carabanchel. The singer began singing *"La chica yeyé,"* which is a song they play on the oldies station. My grandpa, who had just made a little visit to the stand to fill up "the tank," as he calls it, was slowly making his way to the dance floor. People were making way for him, and they looked scared. Nobody dared to compete with that human being.

They formed a circle around him and started clapping. My grandpa threw his beret up in the air and twisted all around like one of those contortionists you see in a circus.

Big Ears said to me, "Your grandpa would look totally cool in a Beyoncé video."

It was true, but how could I tell Beyoncé? I don't have her e-mail or her phone number, and she doesn't come around Carabanchel often.

So, getting back to the dance floor, I could barely see my grandpa because there were so many people around him, not even when Big Ears and I got up on our stools. But this was clearly one of the finest moments of my grandpa's life. And finest moments are almost always ruined by someone. Suddenly I saw a lady who looked kind of familiar elbowing her way through the circle of people around my grandpa. That lady looked familiar because she was . . . my mom! She didn't take my grandpa by the ear, but almost. Our Nosy Neighbor Luisa was with her, and they each grabbed him by an arm and hauled him away, as if they were police officers who had just arrested a criminal. My grandpa resisted arrest. "Please, Cata, darling, I'm begging you. I never leave a party without dancing to *'Paquito Chocolatero'* first."

You probably think *"Paquito Chocolatero"* is some song about chocolate. But it's not. It's this famous *paso doble* some old dude wrote like a hundred years ago.

Everyone knew that without my grandpa there, the party wasn't going to be the same. Big Ears, the Bozo, and I followed the "police officers" as eye witnesses. My grandpa turned around and whispered to me, "Manolito, buddy, do me a favor and stay here to look for my dentures. They got away from me during one of those twirls, and you know I don't want to die without them."

He looked pale, and I felt sorry for him. My mom was so mad that she didn't even realize that Big Ears and I stayed in the park.

I squatted down between all the people to look for his dentures, but since everyone was dancing, they kept stepping on me without thinking twice about it. I told Mr. Ezequiel, the owner of Stumbles and the most powerful person I know, about the dentures, and he took me by the hand and led me up on stage. The music stopped and Mr. Ezequiel said, "Dear friends, at our neighborhood parties people have lost rings, earrings, contact lenses . . . but this is the first time in history that someone has lost dentures. Please take a minute to look around you on the floor for Nicolás Timberlake's smile."

I'll never forget what I saw from the stage: everyone leaned down to look for my grandpa's *smile*.

All of a sudden, Big Ears yelled, "Here they are! I found them!"

Everyone clapped and cheered. I was pretty mad. It's not easy to be happy when your best friend beats you at something.

Big Ears gave the dentures to Mr. Ezequiel, who said, "As president of this neighborhood, I believe that Mr. Nicolás Moreno should receive a medal for shaking it here tonight and for the shaking he's going to get when he gets home."

I said goodnight to Big Ears and headed home,

dentures and medal in tow. When I got to the front door of my building, I called up from the entry phone and my mom said, "What are you doing there? I thought you were in bed!"

Unbelievable. They hadn't even noticed I was gone. It was one of those moments in life when you're not sure whether to be happy or burst out crying.

My parents went to bed. I took the dentures out of my pocket, blew off some of the dirt, and stuck them in the fizzy liquid my grandpa puts them in at night. Then I lifted his head up, put the medal on him, and got into the sofa bed with him.

"Everyone clapped, Grandpa, and Mom will just have to suck it up when she sees you won a medal. It's real bronze, you know."

"Yeah, she's not gonna be happy. But, man, was it worth it, Manol . . ."

His head slumped down on his shoulders. Anyone else would've thought he was dead, but not me, because I know his snoring better than anyone. I see his jaw come unhitched and fall down in front of the TV every afternoon after lunch. Anyway, I think he's immortal. I knew Nicolás Timberlake was just sleeping.

6

A Mermaid in Madrid

Out of nowhere, the phone rang. It was almost 1 a.m. We had all been on the couch sleeping through a movie. Since I don't have to get up early in the summer, they let me stay up till all hours of the night. When the couch began to feel like a sauna, my dad woke up and said, "Man, it's hot. You guys are suffocating me. Bedtime, you leeches!"

That's what my dad calls us. He says we're leeches because we climb up on his stomach and when he's distracted by the TV, we suck his blood. We pretend to, anyway. Without a doubt, the Bozo and I are the two clingiest kids in the worldwide world. Hands down. We love falling asleep on my dad. I used to have my dad's stomach all to myself. Those were the good ol' days. Now I have to share it with the Bozo. Luckily, my dad eats all he can and does his best to increase the surface area of his belly, so there's enough room for the two of us and we don't fight over it. After we've been lying on him for a while and he starts sweating bullets, he yells at us to get off and throws us over on my mom, but he doesn't really mean it because we're his favorite . . . leeches!

So, that night I was telling you about, my dad had tried to peel us off a couple of times; he got mad, but then he laughed when the Bozo stuck his pacifier in my dad's bellybutton. My mom put her feet up on my dad, and he said, "You guys are killing me here. I think I'd be better off in my truck!"

Then the Bozo and I climbed back up on him because we don't like it when he threatens to bolt. It's hard enough having him away Monday through Thursday every week.

"Cata, do something! I can't take it anymore!"

"Good, now you see what pests your children can be," my mom said, moving her feet up closer to his head.

My mom makes these little jokes only on Fridays, when my dad comes home. That's the day when she's in a good mood. My grandpa, who was over at the minibar fixing his famous nightcap, added, "And you're always saying how you don't bond enough with your kids."

It was exactly at that moment, right after my grandpa pronounced those words, that the phone rang. And since it was almost one in the morning, we all jumped. My mom said, "Oh my god. I wonder who died?"

There's no middle ground with my mom: if someone calls at one in the morning, it's because someone just died and they're calling from the funeral parlor. Well, this time she was wrong. It was my super-uncle Nicolás, her brother, who left Carabanchel a year ago and moved to Oslo, the capital of Norway. Now he's getting rich working as a waiter in an Italian restaurant. My uncle's eventually going to be the owner, because he's getting better and better at being Italian. When he calls home from the restaurant, he even speaks with an Italian accent.

My uncle said he was calling so late because he had just asked a Norwegian girl to marry him, and the girl had said yes (in Norwegian), and he wanted to bring her home so we could give our approval.

This was the beginning of the most important experience in my life. You gotta keep in mind that the García Morenos have never married outside of Carabanchel, so this small step was actually a giant leap for our family that was going change the course of history forever.

For the next five days before my uncle arrived, my family was on the verge of having a combined heart attack. Our Nosy Neighbor Luisa and my mom were disinfecting the apartment and the stairs, and they were dusting and shining left and right. I think they even buffed up Bernabé's bald spot.

Finally the big day—A day (A for arrival, of course)—

was here. We all took a taxi to the airport; my mom doesn't like to take the truck to the international terminal because she says they look at you like you're a truck driver. My mom must forget sometimes that my dad's a truck driver. Otherwise I can't understand why she says things like that.

We were almost there. I had been to the airport three times in my life: all three times were to pick up my uncle Nicolás. He's the only relative I have who travels by planes. So whenever I dream about planes and airports, my uncle Nicolás is always in my dream. When I saw with my own glasses the sign that said "INTERNATIONAL," I got scared that the taxi driver wasn't with the program, that he was going to miss it and we weren't going to find my uncle Nicolás. So I grabbed the driver by the back of his head and yelled, "Hey! My uncle from Oslo's coming in over there!"

The taxi driver slammed on the brakes, turned around, and said to my dad, "If you don't tell this little hooligan to calm down, I'll do it myself."

My dad told him, "You can say whatever you want to those three hooligans in that picture up there on your dashboard, but don't you dare say anything to my kid."

And I thought, "My dad's a whole lotta cool."

But that thought didn't last very long, because when we got out of the taxi, my dad grabbed me by the arm and said, "You keep that up, you're going to be grounded the whole time Uncle Nicolás is here."

You can't believe how wild the international terminal

was. There were people from all over. There were little carts to put luggage on, so I grabbed one, because they were free, and I put the Bozo in it, and we zoomed around. Then this guy got right in front of us, and I ran him over. I told him, "I didn't mean it. I didn't mean it," but the guy was ticked and he wouldn't stop complaining to my dad. I think he did it on purpose, just to be mean. And my dad, who gets all stressed out at airports, sided with a stranger for the second time that day and said, "I'm warning you, Manolito: one more strike and you're out."

At that moment, when I was about to cry just to give my dad the satisfaction of seeing how upset he'd made me (he likes us to express our feelings; he doesn't like it when we bottle them up inside), the automatic doors opened and there *she* was, with my uncle not far behind.

My future Norwegian aunt had a really pale face with rosy, chubby cheeks. My uncle, who'd always been a tall uncle in my opinion, came up to her bellybutton, so I came up to her feet. Speaking of feet . . . my future Norwegian aunt's were gigantic. And on top of them were her legs, two mammoth columns that could've held up a Greek temple, and they had really long, really blonde hair on them. My uncle explained to us later that Viking women like things *au naturel*, and they don't wax their legs like my mom does, who has hair just as long, but black.

My future Viking aunt was humongous, the biggest woman I'd ever seen in my life, and we all just stood there looking at her, hypnotized. My uncle, who was grinning

from ear to ear, said, "What do you guys think of my fiancée?"

"She's great, but we don't know where we're going to put her," my grandpa answered.

For the time being, we put her in the taxi, with my grandpa on one side and me on the other. (My parents and my uncle had to take another cab.) My future Viking aunt's skirt hiked up a little bit when she sat down, and you could see her blonde hair. It was beautiful, all sparkly on those huge legs of hers. My grandpa and I stared at her the whole way home. I had to remind myself to swallow every so often. My grandpa would forget and then have to wipe his drool away with his handkerchief.

The whole three days she stayed at our apartment, we didn't take our eyes off her. My grandpa didn't even watch his soap operas. The Bozo and I forgot about our cartoons. We stared at her just like we stare at the TV.

The Bozo was the only one she picked up, lucky guy. I guess it's understandable; she wasn't going to pick up my grandpa, even though my grandpa would've loved to sit on her lap. He kept saying, "Look at this guy—he's only four, and he's already getting all the women!"

By the second day, my mom got a little peeved. She was complaining constantly to my grandpa behind the Viking's back.

"She's a great eater, but she won't step foot in the kitchen."

"Honey," my grandpa said, "you can't expect her to spend the three days she has in Spain cooking."

Since my mom wasn't getting anywhere with my grandpa, she tried my dad: "Don't tell me you think it's attractive for a woman to have hairy legs."

"Cata, they're so blonde, you can't even notice," my dad answered.

Then she whispered to my uncle, "You're mesmerized by her. She'll probably end up leaving you for someone her own size."

"Doesn't she look like a mermaid?" my uncle asked. (He doesn't pay much attention to what my mom says.)

So, finally, my mom came over to me. "You don't have to follow her all around the apartment, you know."

"I'm following her in case she breaks anything in her path. She's so big." It was the only thing I could think of to say.

To wrap things up, my mom took the Bozo from my future Viking aunt and said to him, "Baby's getting a little big to be held all day."

The Bozo just stared at my mom, with that look he gets when he's really mad, and without saying a word, he climbed right back up on my uncle Nicolás's super-fiancée's lap. When the Bozo gets that look on his face, not even my mom dares to challenge him; he could have one of his attacks that make the girl from *The Exorcist* look like a little angel.

A jealous mom can be a terrible thing. A jealous mom is something I don't wish on anyone.

While my mom was going from person to person complaining about all the Viking's faults, I had the three most important days of my life. My uncle let me take her all around Carabanchel—to show the neighborhood off to her and to show her off to the neighborhood. (They didn't have to know she wasn't *my* girlfriend.) She couldn't understand a word I said, but I explained it all with gestures. I would have made a great silent movie actor. Too bad I was born so late.

I told her all the neighborhood secrets: Hangman's Park, the Carabanchel jail (I even told her about the prisoners who go home every night to sleep), the chocolate elephant ears at Ms. Porfiria's store, the *tapas* (tasty appetizers) at Stumbles, and that the cook at Ching-Chong is pregnant with the Chinese waiter's baby, so in six months we'll know what a half Chinchón, half Chinese baby looks like. I showed her my school, and I talked a lot about Ozzy the Bully, about how happy I was that I didn't have to see him all summer. I took advantage of the fact that my future aunt doesn't know bad words in Spanish to insult Ozzy with all the words I know, and she was grinning the whole time. That's the good thing about talking to someone who doesn't understand you; you have more freedom.

Everywhere I took her, she was a success. She did what my uncle Nicolás told her to do: said, "Hi," gave the women a kiss on both cheeks and shook the men's hands, and she made a fantastic impression. My uncle would be a good teacher. He told her fifty times that women get two kisses and men, a handshake. She'd laugh, and my uncle would repeat it again. My uncle told me to tell him when we got back if she'd followed his instructions. I did everything I could to make sure she didn't mess up: when Mr. Ezequiel came out from behind the bar at Stumbles to give her a hug, I warned him, "My uncle Nicolás told her that in Carabanchel, you shake men's hands."

Mr. Ezequiel laughed and said, "Tell your uncle to come down, and he and I will have a little talk about how we do things in Carabanchel."

My uncle came down to Stumbles and ran into some old friends of his from back when he lived in Carabanchel. My uncle talked a lot about Norway, about how it gets dark at three in the afternoon and how the best thing you can do is to get yourself a fiancée like his, because that way you don't get sad even though it's dark out. My uncle Nicolás said Norway was pretty but that he was saving up to eventually open an Italian restaurant in Carabanchel. He said all this without letting go of his fiancée's hand, and I listened to all this without letting go of my future aunt's hand. Both hands, as you have probably realized, belonged to the same Norwegian.

My future Viking aunt coming to town was an event that people in Carabanchel will remember for a long time to come. Even my mom, with all her complaining, has started bragging: "My sister-in-law this, my sister-in-law that." I won't see my future aunt again until next Christmas. On the one hand I wish the summer would never end, but on the other hand I want them to come back. Life's tough.

7

Mustard, My Lifelong Friend

The day before yesterday, at four o'clock in the afternoon, when all of Carabanchel was taking a *siesta* (a crucial part of Spanish culture), the Bozo and I were walking down the street doing our thing. I was giving him advice on life and the different problems and challenges we have to face. The topic we were discussing was: how to eat an ice cream at 4 p.m. in the summertime. Some of you are probably thinking you lick it; others, you bite it. Wow, you're all very smart. But I'd like to see you try and eat an ice cream at 4 p.m., the hottest time of day in my neighborhood in the summer, without getting ice cream all over your clean shirt. It's taken me years of training to figure this out. Now I'm a teacher instructing his pupil.

If you want to sit in a free sauna, just go to Hangman's Park with a towel at 4 p.m. After five minutes you're totally dehydrated, and after ten, you're dead. You're probably wondering how we have survived. Scientists from all over the world have come to my neighborhood to study our strange ability to survive extreme conditions. They were unable to obtain reliable results. However, they did come up with the following hypothesis: "The inhabitants of Carabanchel, Spain, are made of a different mold than the rest of humanity. In the event of a nuclear disaster, the only creatures to survive would be the insects and the inhabitants of this strange place."

I agree with this hypothesis because I prove it every afternoon. After lunch, my grandpa grabs his beret and puts in his dentures and takes us outside. While we walk around eating the ice-cream cone he buys for us at Stumbles, he sits down on the bench in Hangman's Park and snores. He says the heat is good for his bones. Sometimes, when we go to wake him up and we lift up his beret, his head is boiling. You could fry an egg on my grandpa's head. One time some tourists got out of their car, and they took a picture of him while he was sleeping with me and the Bozo on either side of him. Then the tourists got right back in their car because they were about to faint from first-degree burns.

Okay, so I'm giving you all this info to show you that

it's not easy to eat an ice cream at that time of day. As an expert ice cream eater, I have some rules I follow:

1. Eat it quickly.
2. Do not, AT ANY TIME, let it drip.
3. Surprise it with a super lick, before it surprises you with a super stain.

Super stains in my apartment are punishable by a lecture. I've come a long way. A couple of years ago I got a lot more lectures than I do now. And these days I'm also responsible for the Bozo. They never yell at him too much; that's why he goes through life so carefree. The little guy eats his ice cream slowly, sticks his fingers down in the cone and then wipes them on his pants, and he sucks the part of his clothes where the cone dripped. If it's chocolate ice cream, the Bozo turns totally brown (even his underwear); if it's strawberry, he turns pink. The worst part is that sometimes he manages to get it on me, too. Still, he's a happy camper. Me, on the other hand, when I eat an ice cream at 4 p.m., I get real stressed out, thinking about the possible future lectures.

This is what I was talking to the Bozo about the day before yesterday. While I was pouring out advice about how to eat an ice-cream cone, he was covering his whole body with ice cream. So I asked him, "Is the baby understanding any of this?"

"Baby wants with Manolito talking."

That means: "I want to eat my ice cream *and* I want you to keep talking to me" or "Even though I'm not going to pay any attention to you, I like it when you tell me about life." I'm not sure why, but I followed his orders. Well, I do know why: because I'm a good guy and because if I don't, he's capable of throwing a tantrum and waking my mom from her nap. (My mom has a special antenna just for detecting the Bozo's cry; it has a range of several miles.)

I started telling him that I was tired of spending every afternoon with such a little kid like him, that I needed to talk to people from my own generation, that I was tired of all my friends being away on vacation. . . .

"Me, too."

My heart skipped a beat. I looked at the Bozo. I couldn't believe that he had said those words. It's not his style. He always talks in the third person and calls himself Baby. But the one who had really spoken those words was sitting at the window of a ground-floor apartment that's near Stumbles. It was Mustard! Mustard, that kid from my class!

"You wanna come over to my place for a while?" Mustard asked.

What a surprise! The Bozo and I went into the tiny apartment. I had never been there before because it had never occurred to Mustard and me to be friends. I was whispering as I went in; my mom has told us a million times that you have to whisper during *siesta*-time so you

don't wake anyone up. She said when you wake up a mother from her *siesta*, it's a crime against humanity. But Mustard's mom wasn't there since she cleans houses all day, and Mustard's dad left two years ago and they haven't heard from him since. Mustard didn't tell me that; I know it from Our Nosy Neighbor Luisa, who knows everything that goes on in Carabanchel. Sometimes she even finds out what's happening in other neighborhoods. Just to confirm the facts, I asked him, "Where's your mom?"

"Working."

"Your dad?"

"I don't know, and I don't care."

Well, if he didn't care, I didn't either. I was at his home, and my grandpa always says that if you get in an argument with someone at their home, they're right, because it's their home.

So we forgot about his dad and talked about his mom. He told me that one time she cleaned every flight of stairs in the Picasso Tower, which is this super-tall building in Madrid that has twenty-five floors.

Knowing her son, it didn't surprise me: at school we call Mustard the "Atomic Ant" because he's short and speedy. One time he went faster than the speed of light. We timed him and a notary was present and everything. Mustard is the only kid in my class who's shorter than me; that's why I've always been fond of the guy. But Our Teach says that someday Mustard is going to be famous all around the world, not for being short, but for being a great singer. He sings better than the Jonas Brothers and Pavarotti. I really hadn't talked to him that much before; I'd just heard him sing. Mustard doesn't socialize much with my group of friends. He's real quiet, and he only talks to the kid who sits next to him. Our Teach says he does that because he's shy, like all the distinguished men are when they're kids. That means I'll never be a distinguished man. I try to be shy. Sometimes in the morning, I think, "Today I'm going to start being shy. I will be a quiet, interesting kid, a kid who has two or three huge secrets," but no matter how hard I try, it just doesn't come natural to me. As soon as Our Teach asks a question, I'm the first one to raise my hand, whether I know the answer or not. I talk to everyone. I'm a kid with no internal life.

But in the middle of summer, with Carabanchel deserted, Mustard was the only kid I could play with.

"Why don't you ever come to Hangman's Park with us?" I asked him.

"I don't go because you're in Ozzy's gang. Ozzy makes fun of me constantly, and you guys laugh at his jokes."

I told him that Ozzy made fun of me, too, and that I didn't laugh at his jokes. But I was lying. I'm sure Mustard was right. Since Ozzy is always picking on me, I'm glad when he suddenly gives someone else a hard time. I'm only human. And I'm also a bad person. I turned red on the inside, which is a technique I have developed so that people can't tell I'm embarrassed.

"Well, now that Ozzy isn't here, we can make our own

gang," I said to break the tension in the atmosphere. "There's three of us counting the Bozo."

"No, there's four of us."

In Mustard's tiny room was his little sister, Melanie, who must've been the same age as the Bozo.

"Cool," I said to him.

We left the little guys playing Legos while Mustard made two super-chocolate milks and a big bowl of Cocoa Krispies. His tiny apartment was a whole lotta cool.

"You shouldn't pay attention to Ozzy. He's a jerk," I said. I was starting to like this giving-advice thing. "My grandpa says someday I'll be a foot taller than Ozzy. You might not be that lucky; but since you're going to be a famous singer, no one will be able to mess with you, not even Ozzy. Maybe Ozzy will kneel down one day and say, 'Mustard, Mustard, forgive me for everything I've ever done to you. Let me carry your guitar for you. I'm out of work.'"

Mustard laughed really hard at this prediction.

"Before I become a famous singer, I'm going to be a dentist," he told me.

It had never occurred to me to pick a practical profession. Some people's teeth gross me out, but Mustard had his reasons:

"That way, I'll be able to pay for the retainer I need, and I'll have money for my mom to get her cavities filled."

Mustard opened his mouth so I could see how his front teeth stuck out a little bit.

"When I grow up," I said, "I'm going to get rid of my glasses and get blue contacts."

"Cool. You could be an eye doctor and get yourself contact lenses for free."

"Yeah, except for about a month now I've wanted to become a famous actor, you know, internationally and all."

"Well, you can become an eye doctor first, and then when you have your blue contacts, you can look for work as an actor. It's much easier to find a job as an international actor if you have blue eyes, 'cause everyone has brown eyes, and brown eyes aren't going anywhere in life."

"Neat."

Mustard had practical solutions to everything, and there wasn't anything we didn't agree on. I realized we were becoming lifelong friends.

All of a sudden we heard some hair-raising shrieks. They came from the bedroom. We ran in there. The Bozo and Melanie were yanking on each other's hair. They were totally red and still screaming. Mustard grabbed his sister, and I grabbed the Bozo. When we finally pulled them apart, each had a handful of the other's hair. They were breathing hard and glaring at each other.

"She hurt Baby real bad," the Bozo said and burst out crying in my arms.

"He was killing me," said Melanie, and she started crying in her brother's arms.

It took us a long time to get them to go back to playing together. We had to stay and watch them, because every so often one of them would whack the other one accidentally on purpose, and they'd go at it again.

"My sister's got a little temper," said Mustard.

"Yeah, and my brother's a little spoiled," I said.

When we said good-bye, we made them hug. We both knew our terrible pupils were going to have to get along, whether they liked it or not, because they were going to be spending many afternoons together.

Before we left, I asked Mustard, "When you're a dentist, will you make my grandpa some new dentures that stay in place?"

"For sure."

"Meet us tomorrow at four p.m. in Hangman's Park. My grandpa can buy us an ice cream. Since he gets such a small retirement pension, he spends it all on ice cream and things like that."

"He's lucky," said Mustard. He leaned out the window of his tiny, ground-floor apartment to wave good-bye. "I'll have to bring Melanic with me, because my mom doesn't come home until six," he said.

"And I'll have to bring the Bozo, because my mom can't live without her *siesta*."

I can't believe I spent three years in the same class as Mustard without being good friends with him. I'm sure it's because Ozzy the Bully never let him get close to us. Carabanchel without Ozzy was so much cooler! Big Ears was my best friend, of course, but he never thought twice about stabbing me in the back the first chance he got.

Plus, he left me hanging all summer; he hadn't invited me to Carcagente, even though he knew that my parents didn't have any money to take us on vacation this summer.

Now I didn't care if my friends stayed away forever. Without leaving Carabanchel, I had made a lifelong friend.

8

The Return of Big Ears

"**M**anolito . . . guess who!" said the voice on the phone.

"Big Ears!"

Big Ears was back. It had been only a month since he left on vacation, but his voice sounded weird, despite the fact that the other eleven months of the year, we talk on the phone three or four times a day. My mom always says, "Get off the phone! What could you possibly be talking about? You are with each other all day long!" (I'll hang up and the next thing I know, Our Nosy Neighbor Luisa calls, and they spend two hours on the phone talking about stupid stuff. And Luisa lives one floor down! Now, that's what I call teaching by example. The wrong example.)

"I just got back," Big Ears said. "I've been with my dad in Carcagente and then with my mom in Carcagente, and I had an awesome group of friends, and I got to go to the movies for free 'cause my uncle is the guy who takes your ticket on the way in, and one night I stayed up till three a.m. because I was dancing in the Carcagente Ball, which was so much cooler than the one in Carabanchel, and the same girl asked me to dance three times, I swear. The third time I told her, 'I never dance with the same girl three times.' Just like that, those exact words. Where have you been?"

"Here."

"I brought you a jug that says 'I love Carcagente,' and I got Susana a T-shirt that says the same thing. Have you seen Ozzy this summer?"

"Nope. He's been gone, too."

"Dude, you must've been bored out of your mind."

"Not really," I told him.

"Man, time flew by in Carcagente. It was like the days lasted only twenty-two hours, 'cause otherwise it's just not possible for a month to have gone by so fast. I got so much sun, I almost got sick. How about you?"

I was getting sick right then, sick of listening to him. But Big Ears wasn't about to leave me alone. He needed someone to talk to about his dumb summer vacation that nobody cared about.

"I'm going to ask my mom if she'll let me come over to your place for a while," he said.

And his mom let him, of course. His mom lets him do

everything because his parents are divorced. Ten minutes later, Big Ears rang the doorbell. I opened the door, and we stood there staring at each other. He didn't look like my friend. He was all tan and fat. And he was wearing these black sneakers I'd never seen before. That hurts: your friend is away for a month, and when you see him again, he's got new high-tops.

"Do you like them?" he asked, lifting up one foot and then the other. "I got them in Carcagente. They're what Casillas wears in practice."

"How do you know?" It bothers me when people show off like that without having any proof. I don't even like Casillas, even though everyone says he's the best goalie the Real Madrid soccer team has ever had.

"Because I saw him in a magazine the day I got my hair cut at the Carcagente Salon."

Faced with such evidence, I had to keep my mouth shut. I decided to keep my mouth shut for good. I sat on the couch watching TV and didn't say a peep while Big Ears acted all nice to my grandpa, my mom, and the Bozo. His specialty is getting along with all my family members.

My mom called me over in private and said, "But, Manolito, you were dying for Big Ears to come back. All summer long, all you talked about was how bored you were without him, and now that he's finally here, you're totally ignoring him?" When I didn't answer, she walked away, mumbling, "I tell you, this kid is something else."

I went back to my spot on the couch to watch TV. It's just that sometimes you hate your best friend and your mom, and you don't really know why.

Big Ears didn't even care. He wouldn't shut up about the wonders of Carcagente. The worst was the parties:

". . . suddenly I saw this girl coming straight toward me. There were a ton of guys, but she was coming for me, as if no one else in the world existed. I felt bad saying no, so I danced with her once. Then after a little while, she goes and asks me again. I danced with her again because I don't like to be mean."

"And you did the right thing," said my grandpa. "Since the girl was from Carcagente, people would've thought, 'Look at that guy from Madrid, so stuck-up, turning down the best-looking girl in Carcagente.'"

"That's exactly what I thought!" yelled Big Ears, who was excited that my grandpa understood his dilemma. "But then the chick goes and asks me a third time. . . .'"

"And what did you do?" my mom and my grandpa both asked, like it was the most interesting story they'd heard in their lives.

"I said, 'Sorry, I have a rule that I don't dance three times with the same girl.' That's what I said, those exact words."

My mom and my grandpa burst out laughing, and the Bozo clapped. He'd already told me that stupid story. But no one was paying any attention to me. I was acting as peeved as I possibly could, and no one cared.

Big Ears kept on telling us his stories. He told us how

his grandparents on his mom's side don't speak to his grandparents on his dad's side, and they all used him to deliver messages back and forth. He said he was fatter because each of his grandmothers was convinced that at the other grandma's house, Big Ears wasn't fed enough. He showed us his stomach and back, so we could see the terrible effects of the Carcagente sun, but the striptease didn't stop there; to prove how much weight he'd put on and how much he had grown, he told us that he had to buy new underwear, a size bigger. And what do you think he did? He pulled his underwear down a little bit in the back so my mom could check the size on the tag. My mom checked the tag, like she was a judge, and declared for those present: "It is true: this child has gone up a size in underwear."

"No way!" said my grandpa, who was obviously humoring him, too.

Since Big Ears had already pulled down his pants, he decided to show us the difference between his tan back and his white butt. I swear: this kid has no sense of shame. When he spends the night, he walks around our apartment naked, as if it were the most normal thing, or he goes to the bathroom right in front of me. He reminds me of the Bozo. A year ago I decided to start locking the bathroom door, but my mom wouldn't let me because she was scared I would hit my head on the tile and she would have to break down the door to rescue me. A broken door would break my mom's heart. My head being broken would be easier to accept. Anyway, I was tired of everyone opening the door when I was in a state of great intestinal concentration, so I made a sign that my grandpa laminated for me:

DO NOT ENTER!
MANOLITO IS DOING HIS THING

I still use it, and they don't come in. But don't think they do it out of respect for my privacy. They do it out of respect for the smell. Very few humans can stand that aroma. Scientists from all over the world have come to the conclusion that if an individual were to remain in a room full of that type of human gas, he would first lose his mind and then his life. (Unless the individual opened the door and told the scientists that he'd had enough and that the scientists should use their own mothers as guinea pigs. There are individuals that love life too much to sacrifice themselves for a simple scientific experiment.)

But getting back to Big Ears, to the day he returned and how annoying he was: my mom, just to make me mad, invited Big Ears for dinner, but Big Ears said he had to eat all the food his two enemy grandmothers had made for him before it went bad. Thank God. I don't know if I would've been able to put up with him for a whole dinner.

He gave everyone a hug (except me; what next?) and as he was leaving, he said to me, "Manolito, see you tomorrow at Hangman's, right?"

After he was gone, my mom said to my grandpa, "I'm so glad Manolito has Big Ears as a friend!"

They both laughed as they reminisced about the story of the girl in Carcagente, which Big Ears was obviously telling a few times a day.

The next day I went down to Hangman's Park, but I didn't go alone. I asked Mustard to go with me. After all, I'd been hanging out with him every day while Big Ears was away; I wasn't going to ditch him now. (But the true truth is that

I did it to get back at Big Ears.)

Mustard and I sat down on the bench, like every day, watching Bozo and Melanie to make sure they didn't throw dirt in each other's eyes. They're savage children, and you gotta be careful. A little bit later, Big Ears showed up. When he saw the two of us, he just stood there for a second.

"Hey, Manolito, you wanna go to the jail for a while?" he asked.

Big Ears and I like to pretend we're the greatest fugitives of all time, ever since we watched this movie about a guy who wanted to escape from a maximum security prison. During the whole movie, the guy was planning to escape, and when there were only five minutes left and we were finally going to find out if the guy managed to escape or not, my mom got up from her *siesta* and turned off the TV because she said it wasn't an "appropriate topic" for children. I don't know if I've ever told you this before, but right after my mom gets up from her *siesta*, she's in a worse mood than the rest of the day, and that's saying a lot. She usually takes it out on me. That's why she turned the movie off that Saturday, just to be a pain. Ever since then, Big Ears and I have been obsessed with escaping from prison. We like to act this out in the most life-like scene possible, next to the wall of the Carabanchel jail. It's a game that only me and Big Ears play because we're the ones who got stuck without seeing the ending of that movie. So it was no surprise that day when Big Ears, just to get on my good side, suggested we play our secret game.

"So, you wanna go?" he said.

"I can't right now. Me and Mustard are watching the kids."

Big Ears sat down on the bench and didn't say anything. Then I started telling him everything Mustard and I had done since we became lifelong friends. Big Ears was staring at Hangman's Tree, the same way I had been staring at the TV the day before.

"Well, I'm going to go by myself," he said.

I watched him walk away, next to the wall, jumping, running, standing still. . . .

"What's he doing?" asked Mustard.

"He's escaping from a maximum security prison."

That afternoon I waited at home for Big Ears to call, but he was bitter and he didn't. He was obviously deeply hurt that I had another friend. I was hurt that he'd had such a good time in Carcagente behind my back.

"Why don't you call Big Ears, and we can go down to Stumbles for an ice cream?" my grandpa asked.

I stood there next to the phone for about five minutes, debating whether to call or not. When I finally decided to give in, the phone rang. It barely rang once before I picked it up. Guess who it was?

"You wanna come out? You can bring your friend Mustard," Big Ears said.

"No, I'm going out with my grandpa."

"I'm just saying, since you guys are attached at the hip now . . ."

Big Ears and I met up at Stumbles, and my grandpa bought us the ice cream he'd promised.

"Next week school starts. What a bore galore," I said.

"I like the first day. You don't do anything, and you get to see everyone who's back from vacation."

"Except me, 'cause I didn't go anywhere."

"I gotta admit that by the end, I had Carcagente coming out my ears."

"You mean your *big* ears," I said, and we laughed.

"I thought you had an awesome time here with Mustard?"

"Not really. . . . He doesn't know how to play the greatest fugitives of all time."

"That's *our* game. We're the ones who invented it," Big Ears reminded me.

"Next year you could take me with you to Carcagente," I reminded him.

"Or I could stay here with you in Carabanchel."

We started making plans for next summer, a summer when we weren't going to be apart even for a second. We'd spend a few days in one place and then a few days in another, but we'd be together the whole time. Big Ears slept at my apartment that night, and he brought the "I love Carcagente" jug he'd bought for me. The jug was really a piggy bank. We put our first coins in it. We decided to save up for what would be the best summer of our lives: the next one.

9

EGYPTIAN POSE

Presents

I could tell you in detail how Big Ears' birthday went, but you would end up like we did: totally stuffed and fed up. "Stuffed" refers to our bellies; "fed up" refers to our brains.

I will summarize the celebration of the great Big Ears, even though summarizing is not my specialty.

Big Ears' birthday lasted two days. Since his parents are divorced and can't stand the sight of each other, they had two separate parties. The one on Monday was organized by his mom. His friends and relatives were summoned to appear at 6 p.m. at Stumbles, which is where all the kids

in Carabanchel celebrate their birthdays, because Mc-
Donald's is a little out of our way.

Since Big Ears is the only grandchild on his mom's
side, his grandparents came from Carcagente. Big Ears, his
mom, and I went to pick them up at the bus station the
day before the party. Big Ears' grandma couldn't fit
through the bus door; she got totally stuck. The driver
pushed from the inside, and we pulled from the outside.
When we finally freed her, we almost fell down on the
ground in a big pile with the enormous grandma on top of
us. Some grandmothers are deadly.

Once we got over the fright, Big Ears' grandparents-
on-his-mom's-side got ahold of us and planted kisses on us
left and right; our cheeks were red for an hour and a half.
I was sure that they had confused me with Big Ears. It's
not normal for someone to give you so much love the first
time you see them, especially if you consider how little
love some people give me who see me every day.

"Excuse me, there must be a mistake," I said. "Your
grandson is the one with the big ears." (Big Ears got his
grandparents-on-his-mom's-side's ears; it's their family's
number-one trait.)

Big Ears always has one up on the rest of us. His birthday is in September. It's the first birthday of the year, and
all the moms aren't tired yet of giving us money to buy
presents. As the year goes on, the presents go down in
quality and number. By the time Arturo Román's birthday

comes around on June 20, and you go to your mom doing the Egyptian pose, your mom says, "You want money for whaaaaaaaaaat?"

The Egyptian pose has been used for centuries. It's a tradition. You stand in front of a mother, father, or other superior; you turn to the side, place one hand out in front, and wipe all expression off your face. One of two things may happen: you might get lucky and they throw a coin or two in your hand, or the father or cruel mother might totally ignore you and leave you in that pose for hours on end. That's how many Egyptians ended up mummified. (You've probably realized by now that I've got a knack for history.)

The school psychologist came to Big Ears' party, too. His mom invited Miss Espe in case she needed to perform an emergency psychological intervention on Big Ears. And she did: she gave him two lectures, one for not letting us touch his presents, and another for getting up and dancing on one of the tables at Stumbles when Mr. Ezequiel put on a song by Shakira. You should see the skill involved in Miss Espe's lectures. You'd think my mom had given her private lessons. (I don't dare ask Miss Espe because she might decide to give the treatment to me.) Everyone agreed that Miss Espe was the best psychologist in all of Carabanchel and that her methods worked wonders on Big Ears. I, personally, thought the treatment was a little weak for such a wild patient.

The night of Big Ears' birthday, we didn't have dinner

at home because his grandparents-on-his-mom's-side made Mr. Ezequiel fry up some killer *morcilla*, this blood sausage we eat in Spain, which they'd brought from their town. My grandpa said to Big Ears' grandparents, with a piece of the black sausage in his mouth, "This is like a wedding. When I brush my teeth tonight, the water is going to turn black."

"This is pure bliss, Nicolás!" Big Ears' grandpa answered.

The Bozo behaved, in his own way. Every time I looked over at him, he was sitting on a different old person's lap. He didn't have any temper tantrums. On the one hand, he was being a good boy, and on the other hand, he was trying to get as much sausage as he could out of the old people. When we got home and said good-bye to Our Nosy Neighbor Luisa on the stairs, the Bozo let out a deadly fart, one of those silent but violent ones that make their way into your nose with no warning whatsoever.

"Who's the pig in the group?" my mom yelled.

The Bozo raised his hand. He's a guilt-free pig.

It became a matter of utmost urgency, and my mom raced him into Luisa's apartment, since Luisa graciously offered the use of her bathroom. Not a wise move.

We all went into Luisa's bathroom, which is pink and gold and full of really soft rugs and little bottles of aromatic salt so Luisa can take a bath like in the movies. It's a Hollywood bathroom. And there we were, standing there like idiots, waiting for the Bozo to go to work, and him sitting on the throne, like a prince. We saw him turn completely red; his face swelled up like a balloon, and the veins in his neck popped out until suddenly, he went back to his normal state. Then, with great determination and pride, he hopped down from the toilet and pointed.

We all leaned over to take a look, and there was a

general "Oooooh!" upon seeing the result, because it seemed impossible for something so immensely large to have come out of such a small body. It's one of those mysteries that scientists from all over the world have to come to Carabanchel to see. (Many of them, desperate after not being able to find a satisfactory explanation, must retire to a deserted island.)

The *morcilla*—which we'll now call it because of its origin—didn't go down when Luisa flushed.

"Try again," said my mom, getting a little nervous.

Luisa flushed again. We all waited impatiently for the water to stop swirling, to see if we had gotten lucky, but no, our giant *morcilla* was still there.

Luisa and my mom started fighting over which one of them was going to pay for the plumber. Since they couldn't come to an agreement, they decided to take this gross case to the Spanish version of *The People's Court*, you know, that TV show where friends and family go after they've stabbed each other in the back, and there's a trial and a judge decides which party is right, and then they all go home like nothing ever happened. But Bernabé was against my mom and Luisa pulling out each other's hair on national TV, so he put a stop to that and said he would take care of the damages.

The next day, Tuesday, we celebrated the second part of Big Ears' birthday. Big Ears, his dad, and I picked up his grandparents-on-his-dad's-side at the bus station. Man, did they do us in. Big Ears also takes after his dad's parents as far as the ear situation is concerned. The poor guy, he had no chance of getting off the hook, genetically speaking.

The birthday party was at Stumbles again, so we wouldn't break with tradition. The menu was the same as the day before, too. The guests, the same, including Miss Espe, who had to use her lecture treatment twice: when (you guessed it) Big Ears wouldn't let us touch his new toys and when he wanted to get up on the table and lip-sync to Shakira. Big Ears' parents don't like to get their hands dirty lecturing him. That's what the psychologist is for. My mom, on the other hand, loves doing that job. And no one does it better. Why should she hire someone else when she's the best?

After the cake and singing "Happy Birthday" and all that stuff, Big Ears' grandparents-on-his-dad's-side brought out the finishing touch: *chorizo* for Mr. Ezequiel to fry up. *Chorizo* is a real famous Spanish sausage that's red and a little spicy.

"This is like a wedding," my grandpa said to the other grandpa. "When I brush my teeth tonight, the water is going to turn red."

"This is pure bliss, Nicolás!" Big Ears' grandpa answered.

For a second there I had déjà vu.

Before we knew it, it was 11 p.m., but nobody had any intention of leaving, until Mr. Ezequiel said, "All right, friends, Mrs. Ezequiel and I have our limits. We're closing up. Anyone left inside will have to deal with it."

Mr. Ezequiel wasn't kidding. He's left his share of idiots inside all night long. He only gives one warning and then, he closes shop.

Big Ears gathered up his presents. Miss Asunción had given us a talk at school this year about how we should buy educational toys, so I got him a Transformer, but my Transformer looked a little stupid next to the super presents that all his grandparents from Carcagente had gotten him.

While we were walking home, I talked about how Big Ears was so lucky; since his parents are divorced, he gets everything multiplied by two.

My dad said, "Manolito, your mom and I will never get divorced."

My mom grabbed my dad's arm and gave him one of those smiles that make me feel awkward.

"We can't get divorced," my dad went on, "because of the money we still owe on the truck, which we won't be done paying off until the end of this century. So, we'll still be together in the afterlife."

The look on my mom's face turned sour, and her love turned into hate in a matter of seconds. I told you, with my mom, there's only black and white.

When we were going up the stairs, the Bozo started getting mad cramps—to be more specific, when we were on the second floor, Our Nosy Neighbor Luisa's floor. My mom tried dragging him up to our apartment, but the Bozo was clearly not going to take another step. That left my mom with only one choice. She rang Luisa's doorbell and begged her: "Please, a bathroom for this poor child." Luisa wrinkled her nose but let him in.

We all paraded into the famous Hollywood bathroom and huddled around the Bozo. The Bozo inflated like a balloon. There was tension in the air, and danger was brewing. Then he got up, and we saw the present he had left—which we'll call the *chorizo* (because of its origin). My mom said in a very low voice, "Luisa, there's no need to argue. I'll pay for the plumber."

But Bernabé said absolutely not; he would take care of the presents of his godsons until they were of age and could pay for a plumber themselves. I suggested to my mom that, given the frequent problems caused by the Bozo, it might not be a bad idea to take him down to Hangman's Park every afternoon with Miss Bonnie to go to the bathroom there like she does. My mom shot me a hateful look. I decided I couldn't just leave it at that and added, "We can pick it up with a little plastic bag, too."

I ruined it. My mom went into action: she gave me a "delayed-reaction lecture," which means it doesn't really bother me while she's giving it, but after she's done I feel really bad. It's a masterful technique that she uses only on special occasions.

I went to bed thinking that as long as my mother was alive, I wasn't going to make it as a comedian, because she was capable of running up on stage and lecturing me if she didn't approve of a joke. But that wasn't my worst problem that night. I was bitter with envy as I thought about all the presents that were surrounding Big Ears at that very moment.

Luckily, what happened over the next few days made me feel a little better, and my bitter envy turned to sweet envy (although they feel pretty much the same).

But I'm saving that horrific story for the next chapter.

10

Big Ears' Tears

I know you're dying to hear what Big Ears got for his super-duper birthday, but to be honest, I can't remember. There were so many presents! Even now, a few weeks later, Big Ears says that every once in a while he finds unopened packages around his room. You're probably wondering, What does he do with them? Does he open them? No, he doesn't open them, because Big Ears got burned out after so many presents. He said they've only caused him trouble. "What am I supposed to do with so many things? They don't bring me happiness."

And we, his true friends, said all together, "Well, give some to us. Maybe that will solve all your horrible problems."

We're like that in Carabanchel; we only want what's best for our fellow man. But, wait, I don't want to give away the end of the story. I will start this story like always, from the beginning of time.

Everyone knows that Big Ears had two birthday parties, mostly because I told you in the previous chapter of this magnificent book. And everyone knows that his parties made our stomachs churn (because of everything we ate), and he was able to get his hands on thousands and thousands of presents.

The day after his two birthday parties, Big Ears came to school wearing a watch on one wrist with a built-in remote control to turn the TV off and on; on the other wrist, he was wearing a watch with a built-in cell phone; hanging from his pants, he had one of those counters that keep track of how many steps you've taken; he also brought an electric toothbrush for us to try out in class, and everyone used it except Jessica the ex-Fat Fatty, so we're going to start calling her Jessica the Snob. Jessica the Snob said it grossed her out to use a toothbrush that everyone else had put in their mouths.

"But we're from the same class," Arturo Román tried to explain to her. "If a stranger asked you to do it, I'd understand, but not us."

I don't understand people like Jessica, either. I swear, they don't know the meaning of the word "comradeship."

Well, the story didn't end there. Big Ears also had those

sneakers with little lights on the heels that flash when you walk. And then he put on a baseball hat with a green light on the bill, so just in case he was ever lost on some back road, he wouldn't get run over by a car. What does Big Ears do when it gets dark? Simple: he flips the switch and voilà, his hat-light turns on. The only downside is that the people in the car might think he's a UFO and not stop. I'm telling you, between the ears and the green light, Big Ears doesn't look human.

Ozzy the Bully had gone to the dollar store and bought Big Ears a pen. On the pen was a girl in the snow, all dressed up with skis, ready to hit the slopes. But when you turned the pen upside down, the girl's clothes disappeared and she was left there wearing just her skis. I felt bad that the poor girl was naked in such a cold place, but then I thought, "Aw, it's all fake, anyway, like car chases in the movies," and I turned the pen upside down about sixty times in one minute.

Oh! Big Ears also brought in a calculator with an alarm clock. Just in case he falls asleep in the middle of a math problem on a test. Don't laugh: Big Ears is capable of doing it. He says division problems that have more than two digits have a drowsy effect on him. He can't understand why some people have trouble sleeping when you can just sit down with a math problem. He says just looking at a math problem makes his ears itch. And when Big Ears' flaps start itching, a minute later he's out for the count.

So anyway, when Our Teach came through the door that morning, she had to take off her reading glasses and put on her far-away glasses just to confirm what her eyes were witnessing. There was envy floating in the air. It was an envy so thick that we couldn't see the person in front of us. That day, everyone would have liked to sit next to Big Ears, but they had to suck it up, because the person who sits next to Big Ears is *me*: in good times and in bad, in sickness and in health, when you have to hold a handkerchief up to his bloody nose, when he falls asleep on your shoulder, or when you have to let him copy an entire exam, from start to finish. There have been times when he's copied so well that he's written my name at the top instead of his own. But Miss Asunción recognizes Big Ears' handwriting (there's no mistaking it), and she immediately slaps a big fat F on his paper.

That day, Miss Asunción gave us some killer problems to solve: five division problems, all with more than two digits. Sometimes I wonder, "How is it possible for so much cruelty to fit into one teacher?" I bit my lip like I always do when I'm racking my brain (if I don't, I can't think). Then I saw that Big Ears, instead of copying, was smiling. He had taken his alarm clock-calculator out of his desk and was solving all the problems. It was awesome. So we both wrote down the answers without having to do all the work, which is a booooore.

Since we had so much time left, I asked Big Ears to let me see the skier-lady pen, and we undressed her and showed Paquito Medina, who sits behind us. Five minutes later, Arturo Román and Oscar Mayer, who sit behind Paquito, had stopped doing the assignment and were nearly standing up, trying to catch a glimpse of the skier-lady.

Our Teach came over, clicking her heels on the floor even harder than normal just to terrify us, and since I was

the one holding the pen, she said, "Manolito, what do you have there that's so interesting?"

"A pen . . ." I said, and I began praying for my life.

When she grabbed the pen out of my hands, the girl's clothes fell off. Miss Asunción had to take off her far-away glasses and put back on her reading glasses to see better.

"Manolito, where did you get this?"

"It's not mine. It's Big Ears'."

"I didn't buy it. Ozzy gave it to me," said Big Ears.

"I bought it for him because Mustard has one just like it, and Big Ears said he wanted one for his birthday," said Ozzy.

"Yeah, I have one just like it," said Mustard, "but I never turn it upside down."

No one was stupid enough to believe *that*.

We pointed fingers at each other for a good while until Our Teach finally came to the conclusion that we were all guilty. She put the pen away and said in a mysterious tone that she would "take measures."

She continued with her police bust: She saw the alarm clock-calculator in between our papers and informed us that we were going to get a zero for those problems. Then she gave us such a long speech that I've forgotten most of it, except the part where she said calculators should be forbidden at school, just like cell phones and tattoos.

After our zero in math, we moved on to science. Our Teach took us to the auditorium, where they were showing a documentary on TV about the reproduction of rodents. She said that this way, we could skip the chapter about human reproduction, a chapter we didn't get to finish last year because we couldn't stop giggling.

While we were walking down the hall, Big Ears called his dad from his cell phone-watch to tell him what was being served for lunch that day, and a minute later his dad called back to tell him to chew his steak really well, so what happened last year wouldn't happen again (Big Ears almost had to be carried out of the cafeteria, feet first).

When we walked into the auditorium, the phone rang two more times: the first time was his grandma-on-his-mom's-side from Carcagente, who wanted to say "hi" to Miss Asunción, and the second time it was Big Ears' mom, who was calling to tell Big Ears not to talk on his cell phone at school. Well, he couldn't have talked anymore on it, because at that moment, Our Teach confiscated it. She turned off the light so we could watch the documentary, and Big Ears thought that was a good time to play around with his hat. He hit the switch, and the bill turned off and on. The green light was a whole super-lotta cool. The whole class went, "Oooooh!" Our Teach thought we were ooohing and ahhhing at the documentary, and she turned around from her front-row seat to yell, "You better not start up like last year!"

But she realized we didn't give a rat's tail (no pun intended) about the rodents because we were all looking at Big Ears' lit-up head. So she took away his hat, too, and a little while later the alarm clock-calculator, which was programmed to play "Happy Birthday" every hour. Our Teach got peeved because when we heard the music, we all started singing. You try listening to "Happy Birthday" without singing. Impossible. Even if someone sealed your lips shut with super-adhesive tape, you'd keep singing mentally. Scientists threw in the towel long ago while researching this strange process.

The straw that broke the camel's back (or Our Teach's back, in this case) was when Big Ears pressed the remote control on his watch and the TV changed channels. All of a sudden, we went from watching rodents to watching a game show. Ozzy whistled at a pretty girl on the show, and we all joined in. Miss Asunción yelled at Big Ears to change the channel back. Big Ears hit all the buttons trying desperately to change it back, but the pretty girl wouldn't budge. We kept on whistling, because the girl really deserved it, and Our Teach yelled even louder at Big Ears to turn it off. But Big Ears didn't know how. He was almost crying when he asked if he could call his dad for help. Our Teach said in a very dramatic voice, "*I* will call him."

You should've seen Miss Asunción trying to follow the instructions from Big Ears' dad. She was biting her lip just like I do when I'm attempting division problems.

After that, all of Big Ears' electronic devices were taken away from him until the day comes when he is psychologically prepared to use them. If we really wait for that day to come, Big Ears will never see those gadgets again. That's why he confessed to us at Hangman's Park, with tears in his eyes, "Why do I want so much stuff, if it doesn't bring me happiness? If they say I don't have enough common sense to use it?" And we all offered to help him by taking the presents off his hands.

But then Big Ears, with one of his big smiles, said, "Now that I think about it, there is something about these presents that brings me happiness."

"What?" we all said together.

"The fact that you guys don't have them."

And his tears of sadness turned into tears of joy.

11

Life's Tough

I had to wash my feet this morning. I've had to wash them every morning for the past few weeks. And that's not even the worst of it. I have to wash them at eight in the morning. That's how brutal my existence has become. I don't do it because I enjoy it. (What'd you think, I was one of those weird guys who wash their feet without anyone making them?) I do it because school's started. I know, you're thinking, "Yeah, but school started every other year, and your mom got on your case about bodily hygiene, but you managed to get out of it, Manolito. Nobody can accuse you of taking a shower every day."

It's true, but what happened is that last year, before she let us out for summer vacation, Miss Asunción told our parents that the mix of sweat from our bodies was dangerous and volatile, and there were times, like when we'd come back in from recess, when she thought she was going to faint. Our Teach also said that some days in the winter, when we had all the windows shut real tight to keep out the cold, the body odor (otherwise known as B.O.) that our bodies gave off was actually visible over our heads, like the gray cloud that's over Madrid because of all the pollution, which we learned about last year. As you can see, Miss Asunción takes advantage of every insult to teach us and of every lesson to insult us. She gives us a complete education.

Our Teach went on to say that if the problem didn't get resolved, our parents were going to have to buy her a gas mask and some oxygen tanks just to recycle the air every once in a while. She says we don't need to have new air because we're mutant kids. Like the fish in the pond at Retiro Park that are used to eating the gum all the kids in Madrid throw in there, we can adapt to a putrid environment.

Miss Asunción ended her speech by consoling our parents: "In all other regards, they're great kids, especially during the three months they're on vacation." And having said that, Our Teach turned and walked out the door, laughing at her witty remark.

When she has us nearby, she likes us less. That's what it seemed like on the first day of school. You couldn't get a smile out of her, and we did a lot of funny stuff, but there was no way. She doesn't share our sense of humor.

So, anyway, this year my mom wants it to be clear to everyone in Carabanchel and the worldwide world that the other kids are the filthy ones, not her son. She's determined to make me squeaky clean before I go to school; so not only do I have to take a shower every night, which would be the normal thing to do, but I also have to prepare for morning inspection, too. (And I used to have so much fun picking out the little lint balls between my toes while I watched my favorite TV show. Try it: it's really relaxing. It's recommended by psychologists all over as a great stress-reliever.)

But not all the surprises were bad ones at the beginning of the school year. A couple of days before school started—which from now on will be referred to as D day (D for dreaded)—I found out that my mom had signed the Bozo up for a preschool class at my school. Preschool consists of a group of little kids spending all day playing and singing and sleeping, while the teachers elbow each other and say, "How naïve! They think this is what school is like! They have no idea what's in store for them. Ha ha ha." There are teachers who should star in horror films.

I was really excited that the Bozo was going to school with me. It's no fun to have to go off with your feet washed and your backpack weighing you down, to that form of torture they call "school," while your dear little brother waves good-bye from Mommy's arms with his pajamas still on. That hurts. And the crazy part is that the Bozo wants to be just like me. He spent all last year pretending he was going to school every morning. The truth is, the only thing the two of us have in common is our last name.

Back to what I was saying, this year I wasn't the only loser who left the García Moreno residence on D day. A new member of the Clean Feet Tribe joined me: the Bozo.

He had a backpack, too. Of course, it was nothing like mine. Mine had serious stuff inside: new books that would torture my brain for months. In his backpack, my mom had put some tissues for his snot, a backup pacifier just in case he had a sudden temper tantrum, and a change of pants in case he decided that the bathroom at school was too far from his classroom.

My grandpa took us to school, and we were late. No surprise there. Everyone wanted to give the Bozo advice on his first day (they couldn't care less about me). Our Nosy Neighbor Luisa and my mom blew him kisses from the window. Mr. Ezequiel waved good-bye to him from Stumbles. Ms. Porfiria even gave him a chocolate elephant ear from her store, and that is something that will go down as one of the major events of the twenty-first century, because Ms. Porfiria has rules and she never ever bends them. You can read them for yourself on a sign outside the store:

> *In this establishment, there is no layaway, no giving away, no discounting, no nothing.*
> *—Porfiria's*

The Bozo looked like the king of Spain, waving left and right, loving his position at the center of the universe.

I thought, "Enjoy it while it lasts, little one."

I thought he was going to cry when we got to school, like any civilized kid would do in such a dramatic situation. But the Bozo's reaction was unpredictable, like always. I thought he would do what any other novice would do in his place: grab onto a streetlamp or a bench—or throw himself on the ground as a last resort—what all kids have done on their first day of school since the beginning of humanity. But not the Bozo. He said good-bye to my grandpa with one of his killer smiles and walked in through the door like it was no big deal. One thing, though: there was no convincing him that the elephant ear was for snack time.

"Baby wants his ear now."

"Well, Baby's going to have to suck it up because here they don't let you eat until snack time," I said. I'm an expert in school rules (and not exactly because I've studied them).

The Bozo looked at me like, "How stupid. Who made up that rule?" He looked at me just like that, I swear. The Bozo's vocabulary is limited, but his thoughts are pretty deep. A lady took him by the hand to lead him to his classroom, but he pulled his hand away and explained to her, in a completely calm voice, "Baby wants go with Manolito."

"You can go with your brother later, at recess," she said and took him away with a smile on her face that reminded me of a nurse leading a crazy person into an insane asylum.

When I got to my classroom, Miss Asunción greeted me with the same affection as always: "First day, and you're late. You're off to a good start, Manolito."

Ten minutes later, she had us doing division problems to show the worldwide world just how much we'd forgotten from the year before and that we'd spent the summer relaxing, picking out the little lint balls from between our toes, and that we hadn't done a single math problem she'd sent home for us to do. She's a masochistic teacher: she likes to see that her orders go in one ear and out the other. She's also a sadistic teacher: she likes to make us suffer right from the first minute of the first day of the school year. To be exact, she's a sadomasochistic teacher. (Paquito Medina taught me those words.) She's got it all. But I don't mean to criticize, because I don't like talking bad about people.

Well, there I was biting my tongue while I was doing one of the division problems that totally demoralize you, when the door opened and a kid about four years old with a backpack came in. The kid went up to Our Teach and said, like it was the most normal thing in the world, "Baby wants go with Manolito."

And then the kid went and stood next to me. That kid with the backpack, as you've probably guessed by now, was none other than the Bozo. Miss Asunción came over to us. "Manolito, take your brother to his classroom."

Easier said than done. Miss Asunción didn't know how hard it is to change the Bozo's mind. Just wait till he's her student. She'll longingly think of me and say, "I complained about *Manolito*! Now I realize what a sweetheart with glasses he was."

So, there was the Bozo. He had escaped from his classroom and had no intention of letting anyone separate us. You are probably all wondering, "What did Manolito do at that critical moment?" It wasn't easy, you'll agree with me on this one, but I'm a resourceful kid. I whispered something in his ear, and then he stared at me for a minute, and at last he decided to go back to his classroom. Before he left the room, his teacher came rushing in, out of breath and looking pretty scared. No teacher likes to lose a kid on the first day of school. It doesn't leave a good impression on the parents.

The Bozo stayed for a few more minutes waving good-bye to everyone, and my whole class waved to him, too. Both of our teachers let him take his time saying good-bye. I don't know how he manages to get all of humanity on his side.

Our Teach asked me, "Manolito, what'd you whisper to him?"

"That you come to school to learn, and you have to obey your teacher." Yes, believe it or not, those words actually came out of my mouth.

Miss Asunción walked slowly back to her desk, but

she didn't take her eyes off me for the rest of the morning. I think she kept pinching herself to make sure she was awake and had really heard those surprising words. She doesn't think a kid like me can come back from vacation totally reformed. She doesn't believe in miracles.

But the Bozo's little scenes didn't stop there. When it was time for recess, his poor teacher came over to me looking worried again and told me that my brother had been swinging for an hour and wouldn't let anyone else have a turn. When I got to the preschool playground, I witnessed an unfortunate sight: the Bozo was swinging like crazy and laughing at the top of his lungs, while the other kids were pointing at him and pouting because they had been waiting so long for their turn to swing.

At that moment, I felt like the policeman that everyone is counting on to have a talk with the criminal. It was a very delicate situation, as you can see.

"Stop for a sec, I want to tell you something!" I shouted.

The Bozo put his feet down and stopped but didn't let go of the swing. All the kids watched.

I whispered something to the Bozo, and he immediately jumped off the swing.

"What did you say to him?" his teacher asked me.

"That you can't do that, that at school you learn to be generous and share." As you can see, I was getting better and better at playing the reformed kid. "The problem is my mom really spoils him, and then he acts like a savage.

I always have to make peace wherever he goes."

"Thanks, Manolito," said his teacher. Not to brag or anything, but I was turning into her hero and it was a pretty nice feeling. Since the school year began, I've had to step in on five different occasions: once, because the Bozo was giving his elephant ears to the maintenance guy's dog (he's only generous with animals); a second time, because he wouldn't stop lifting up the skirt of this girl in his class (my mom and Our Nosy Neighbor Luisa laugh when he does it to them, and he doesn't understand why all women don't like it); a third time, because he kept dipping his pacifier in the water they were using to dip their paintbrushes; a fourth time, because he wouldn't come out of the bathroom; a fifth time, because he kept singing a different song than the one the teacher asked the class to sing.

As you can see, his teacher, Miss Estrella (that's the victim's name), and I have become pretty close. After all, we share a common impossible mission: the Bozo's education.

Well, I'll end this final chapter by telling you the real truth, which is much sadder:

I would never tell the Bozo all that stuff about generosity and sharing or anything like that. The Bozo could care less about that, and not because he doesn't understand it, but because no one could ever get him to do something based on those arguments. The only way to get the Bozo to do something—and I know because I know the Bozo better than his own mother—is to go after his weakness. And his weakness has a name: Ms. Porfiria's pastries.

To get him to leave my classroom, I promised him my donut the next day, and to get him off the swing, I promised to give him my elephant ear the day after that. So far, I have promised him my snack for the next two months. Seeing how things are working out and the criminal history he's managed to establish in such a short period of time, it's quite possible I will be without a snack for the entire year. And they say I don't love my brother! I'm capable of giving up my favorite things just to make a civilized kid out of him. That's how tough life is.

Well, there's one more small piece of truth I've kept to myself: I've also been making those sacrifices so that the Bozo's pretty teacher doesn't lose her admiration for me. It's the best thing that's happened to me in my planetary life.

It makes me want to be six years younger so I can be in her class or fifteen years older so I can wait for her outside school. When I told this to my grandpa, he wasn't surprised. He said he'd already noticed her, and that he liked her, too.

"But she's too young for me and too old for you, Manolito," he said.

My grandpa's the only one who knows how much I like Miss Estrella. I like her better than any pastry Ms.

Porfiria makes, just to give you an idea. So, I'm asking you not to tell anyone. I don't want the kids in my class making fun of me.

And most of all, I don't want to ruin my new role in life: hero.

ELVIRA LINDO's series about the adventures of Manolito Four-Eyes is a children's classic in Spain, where it has inspired feature films and a TV series, and is also popular in other European countries. She has received Spain's National Children's Book Award, and her books are regularly translated into some twenty languages. She also works as a screenwriter, and her weekly column in *El País* newspaper is widely read in Spain and Latin America. She lives half of the year in New York City.

EMILIO URBERUAGA is a writer and illustrator in Spain whose work has been published all over the world.

CAROLINE TRAVALIA, Ph.D., is an assistant professor of Spanish at Hobart and William Smith Colleges in New York. In addition to Spanish language, she teaches Spanish linguistics, translation, and children's literature. She has published articles on topics including Spanish expressions and colloquial Spanish language.